THE FRENCH RESISTANCE

THE FRENCH RESISTANCE

By Don Lawson

Julian Messner
New York

Published by JULIAN MESSNER
A Division of Simon & Schuster, Inc.
Simon & Schuster Building
1230 Avenue of the Americas
New York, New York 10020

Designed by Prairie Graphics
Manufactured in the United States of America

10 9 8 7 6 5 4 3 2 1

JULIAN MESSNER and colophon are trademarks
of Simon & Schuster, Inc.

SPY SHELF BOOKS is a
trademark of Simon & Schuster, Inc.
Also available in Wanderer paperback edition

Library of Congress Cataloging in Publication Data

Lawson, Don.
   The French Resistance.

   (Spy shelf)
   Summary: Describes the French Resistance, the underground movement which through undetected acts of
sabotage, intelligence gathering, and willingness
to risk their lives, insured countless German defeats
and strongly influenced the outcome of World War II.
   1. World War, 1939–1945—Underground movements—
France—Juvenile literature. 2. France—History—
German occupation, 1940–1945—Juvenile literature.
3. Guerrillas—France—Biography—Juvenile literature.
[1. World War, 1939–1945—Underground movements—
France. 2. France—History—German occupation, 1940–
1945] I. Title. II. Series.
D802.F8L365   1984   940.53'44   83-1124
ISBN 0-671-46775-1
ISBN 0-671-50832-6 (lib. bdg.)

Contents

FOREWORD:

My

Counterintelligence

Days

DURING WORLD WAR II, I served in England and France with the Counterintelligence Branch of the United States Ninth Air Force headquarters. The most exciting part of our work was with the French underground, or resistance, though it was only after the war was over that we could fully realize the true immensity of the resistants' power and influence.

We were always aware, of course, of the French underground and its willingness to risk everything to win the war. But while those crucial years of the war were passing, I had countless questions that remained unanswered.

I often wondered why the Luftwaffe always seemed to be surprised by the introduction of new American planes into combat. In England we prepared intelligence summaries for our fighter and bomber squadrons. These summaries included the latest information on German Luftwaffe aircraft as well as a listing of the aerial tactics which had proved most effective against them.

We also briefed newspaper war correspondents on what specific information they could use in filing stories about U.S. Air Force combat planes and missions. When a new American plane was introduced into the European Theater of Operations (ETO), for example, no mention of it was allowed in dispatches until a minimum of three of the new planes had been shot down over enemy territory. By then, it was assumed, the enemy would have learned enough about the new aircraft to permit its being mentioned in news stories.

Both the U.S. P-63 Black Widow and P-51 Mustang fighters had scored many combat victories before the Germans seemed to become generally aware of their presence. When the German counterintelligence service finally issued intelligence summaries about these new aircraft, they were weeks and even months late and must have been of only limited use to the Luftwaffe.

These enemy intelligence summaries were smuggled to us by resistance agents, many of them French. They also smuggled out information about new German aircraft and terror weapons long before they were actually operational, so our intelligence summaries alerted our fliers before the fact, not after it. Our combat crews, for example, were looking for the first German jet fighter plane long before they actually encountered it near the end of the war. And, again thanks to information supplied by the underground resistance on the continent, both the Eighth and Ninth U.S. Air Forces as well as the British Royal Air Force (RAF) had run numerous bombing missions against the V-1 and V-2 rockets and pilotless buzz-bomb sites months before these aerial weapons went into use.

Didn't the Germans have any agents or spies in England who could supply their combat forces with the same kind of information we were getting from our resistance agents? It seemed impossible that they wouldn't have. I didn't really get an answer to that question until long after the war. You will find it in Chapter IV, "Secret Agent Operations."

One of our more interesting jobs in counterintelligence was briefing our aircraft crews on escape and evasion techniques they should use if they were shot down over France and wanted to avoid being captured by the Germans. By the time the United States got into the war the French resistance movement had established regular escape routes along which escaping Allied fliers could be smuggled out of France, down into Spain, and back to England. These are told about in this book's chapter, "Escapees and Evaders."

One of the most informative counterintelligence techniques we exercised in England was debriefing downed American fliers who had escaped from France. What we were interested in, of course, was how they had evaded capture, where they had been rescued by the resistance, and how they had been passed along the escape network. New escape and evasion techniques could then be given to our combat aircrews.

Later on in the war, when the Allies had successfully invaded Normandy, we set up headquarters in a building at Chantilly, which was one of the camouflage wonders of the war. It had previously been occupied by the German Luftwaffe fighter command headquarters, but we did not know that until a few days before we took it over. In fact while we were still in England, Allied intelligence had been trying for months to locate it so it could be bombed.

We constantly kept getting reports from the

French resistance that the German fighter command headquarters was located in the forest surrounding Chantilly, but numerous low-level aerial photographic reconnaissance missions failed to disclose it. All that showed up on the photos were trees. When we finally arrived on the scene we saw why.

Even at ground level it was impossible to see the building we were guided to until we were almost on top of it. This was because a huge net the size of a circus tent had been spread over the sprawling, modernistic one-story structure and on top of this net fresh-cut sod had been placed. On top of the sod young saplings and fairly good-sized trees had been fastened. Later we learned that every few weeks the sod and trees were replaced so no telltale signs of brown amidst the green of the surrounding forest would show up in aerial photographs. To this day I marvel at the incredible effort and efficiency that had to go into this transplanting effort, which was always accomplished in one night's time.

It was from this headquarters—it was not necessary to maintain its camouflage cover because the Allies had complete control of the air—that I made frequent trips into the surrounding towns and villages to conduct interviews with former resistance members. (They flatly refused to come to the hated *Boches'* headquarters even though it was now occupied by Americans.) I was immediately involved in collecting valuable information about several French men and women who had collaborated with the enemy during the German occupation of France. But most interesting of all were the dramatic experiences the local resistance leaders had to tell about their own experiences as members of the resistance. Many of these stories have been woven into this book.

During the course of these interviews I began to realize just how little I actually knew about the French resistance movement, how it began, its size, its overall activities. Up to now my view had been too close-up, too much a matter of looking at bits and pieces, to see the resistance operation as a whole.

Such is true, of course, of all intelligence and counterintelligence work. Most of it by its very nature is necessarily conducted on a "need to know" basis, so that only those who must have it to perform their wartime jobs are given secret information. How many people right on the scene, for example, knew about what was probably the most important single Allied intelligence coup of the war—the cracking of all the German military codes following the capture of the Enigma coding machine? (See Chapter IV, "Secret Agent Operations.'') I certainly had no inkling of this aptly designated "Ultra Secret" until long after the war, and yet during the war "Ultra" messages must have been constantly going out of our headquarters—but only to top Air Force commanders.

In fact, despite my direct involvement with intelligence, counterintelligence, and the French resistance during the war, my lack of knowledge was so great that my own "need to know" continued after the war. My interest in the subject has grown ever since, and this book is one of the results.

—D. L.

I

The Launching
of the Underground

WORLD WAR II began on September 1, 1939, when Germany invaded Poland. By the following spring Adolf Hitler's armies and air force had conquered much of Western Europe and had driven France's ally, the British, from the continent. On June 14, 1940, the German military juggernaut rolled into Paris. On June 17 Marshal Henri Philippe Pétain, France's prime minister, asked the Germans for surrender terms.

Hitler's terms were harsh. The French were allowed, however, to set up a puppet government at Vichy in the unoccupied southern third of the country.

Marshal Pétain frankly declared that his government at Vichy would openly collaborate with the Germans. Nevertheless, unoccupied France became a haven for thousands of refugees fleeing the enemy-occupied zone. There were no German troops there and, for a few months, French civilians were able to live more or less normally.

Those who remained behind in Paris and the rest of occupied France were initially surprised at how well behaved and considerate the conquering Germans were. They committed no atrocities. On the contrary, they went out of their way to be friendly with the French. More importantly, they even set up food depots and soup kitchens to feed everyone until the war-disrupted economy could be brought back to normal. The general atmosphere of numb disbelief that immediately followed the fall of France was soon replaced by a feeling of relief that the fighting was over. Perhaps their conquerors weren't such bad people after all. Collaboration with the conquerors soon became the only sensible way of life to many of the practical French people.

But not by any means to all of them.

The First Signs

The first acts of resistance were small ones, like those committed by students trying to annoy a tyrannical teacher. Germans seeking directions on the Paris Métro (subway) would be misdirected to stations beyond their destination. When Germans entered a restaurant or other public place, all of the French men and women would get up and leave. Anti-German graffiti began appearing on the walls of Paris buildings. In the Jewish section of the city this graffiti took the form of the Mogen David, or six-pointed Jewish star, drawn on German propaganda posters. This defacement of their posters was especially irritating to the anti-Semitic enemy.

In many parts of Paris bumper stickers were also used effectively. Few French citizens were allowed to drive automobiles, but the Paris streets were usually filled with German vehicles. When they were left unattended for a brief time, bumper stickers would mysteriously appear on them bearing the legends, "V pour Victoire," or "Vive la France," or "Vive de Gaulle."

Although Great Britain had been driven from the Continent, it had not been driven out of the war. Britain's Prime Minister Winston Churchill adopted the V for Victory symbol as his own personal sign of defiance against the Germans, and soon it spread throughout occupied Europe. To the V for Victory symbol the French often added their own Cross of Lorraine. This cross stood for both the promised liberation of the German-held

French province of Lorraine as well as for the liberation of the whole of France. Charles de Gaulle, who himself became a symbol of a defiant France, soon adopted the Cross of Lorraine as the emblem for the Free French movement outside Paris.

De Gaulle's Rallying Cry

De Gaulle, a tank corps officer whose faith in the eventual defeat of Germany never wavered, had left France on the eve of the German occupation. He had not left through fear of capture but because he refused to take part in Pétain's surrender. Pétain had de Gaulle charged with desertion and ordered him shot if he returned to France. De Gaulle fled to England, where on the very eve of France's capitulation he broadcast a message of hope, not despair, to the French people. Few French citizens actually heard the historic broadcast, but those who did spread its message throughout the country. De Gaulle's challenge did much to rally the French people and helped spark the real beginnings of the resistance movement.

In his broadcast de Gaulle said, in part: "Is the last word said? Has all hope gone? Is the defeat definitive? No. Believe me, I tell you that nothing is lost for France. This war is not limited to the unfortunate territory of our country. This war is a world war. I invite all French officers and soldiers who are in Britain or who may find themselves there, with their arms or without, to get in touch with me. Whatever happens, the flame of French resistance must not die and will not die.''

Many French people had never even heard of Charles de Gaulle. But from that point forward he became their true leader. All over France a new symbol began to appear. It simply showed two sticks with the French words *Deux Gaules*, meaning "two sticks" but pronounced exactly like de Gaulle.

The great difficulty for potential resistants, as they came to be called, was in forming any kind of organization. In the beginning potential resistants hesitated to mention their feelings for fear they might be talking to a collaborator who would want to win favor with the Germans and report the conversation.

This problem was solved by cautiously sounding out one's friends and neighbors regarding their political views. If their response was pro-German, the subject was dropped. If anti-German, the idea of active resistance was pursued. This technique was widespread, but it was used especially effectively by Henri Frenay, who organized one of the first resistance groups, called Combat.

The First to Die

But before any regular resistance organizations were formed, many French people engaged in acts of sabotage individually. One of these early saboteurs was a young man named Etienne Achavanne, whom historian David Schoenbrun has called "the first martyr of the resistance." In June of 1940 young Achavanne cut the telephone lines leading into an airfield near the town of Boos. As a result the airfield was without communications and could not be warned by Luftwaffe interceptor headquarters of an imminent Royal Air Force bombing raid. Scores of German soldiers were killed and numerous aircraft were destroyed in the surprise RAF raid.

A short time later a teenager named Pierre Roch performed a similar feat in western France, and soon telephone cables carrying military traffic were being cut throughout the country.

Both Achavanne and Roch were caught and publicly executed. Up until this time minor acts of resistance had been punished with arrests and fines. But now the Germans announced that harsher measures would be used, including the taking of hostages who would be shot when any act of resistance was performed.

Despite this grim warning, the students at Paris University and several other colleges in the city decided to stage a protest demonstration on November 11, the traditional day for celebrating the armistice that ended World War I. On November 10 notices appeared in the Paris newspapers forbidding any observance of Armistice Day. Nevertheless, the students continued with their plans to demonstrate.

On the morning of Armistice Day several thousand students marched to the Arc de Triomphe, where they placed a wreath on the Tomb of the Unknown Soldier and hoisted the tricolor, France's national flag. The police then tried to get the crowd to disperse. This the students refused to do. Instead they linked arms and began singing the French national anthem, "La Marseillaise."

Soon the crowd of students swelled as other patriotic French men and women joined the noisy demonstrators. The police continued their dispersal efforts. When these failed, a company of German infantry came out of a nearby movie theater where they had been stationed in case of emergency. First the soldiers fired over the heads of the crowd. Then they fired into it. Several grenades also exploded. The demonstrators then fled, leaving behind them at least a dozen dead and an unknown number wounded. Several hundred arrests were also made.

Resistance Begins to Grow

The violent German reaction to this relatively peaceful Armistice Day celebration by unarmed demonstrators gave new impetus to the resistance movement. Within a matter of days hundreds of students were planning to form resistance organizations of their own or began seeking already-formed organizations they could join. They had not far to look, for one such group had already become active right within Paris. This was formed by a group of anthropologists at the Musée de l'Homme (Museum of Man). Within a matter of weeks this group would publish the first underground newspaper to appear in Paris. Fittingly, the newspaper was called *Résistance*. Soon its mimeographed pages were distributed throughout the city by rebellious students willing to risk their lives to recruit followers to the anti-German cause.

Elsewhere in France several other resistance

organizations had also begun to form. Having learned how effective disrupting telephone communications could be, telephone workers began to form a clandestine operation—not only to sabotage military calls but also to intercept important messages and pass them along to British spies. Soon postal workers also realized the key role they played in the communications network, and they too began a silent campaign of intercepting vital messages. Railroad workers, who were among the few French people allowed to travel freely throughout the country, became valuable messengers, especially between the occupied and unoccupied zones.

As soon as they took over most of France (except for Vichy), the Germans began to build fortifications along the English Channel coast. Realizing how important plans for these fortifications would be to the British as well as to General de Gaulle's fledgling Free French movement in London, a French resistance group was formed to obtain details of Hitler's Atlantic Coast defenses. This invaluable organization was led by Gilbert Renault, who would soon become widely known by his code name of Colonel Rémy.

In order to build these fortifications the Germans seized many French civilian men and put them into forced-labor battalions. This led to one murderous act of retaliation against the Germans that became famous throughout occupied France.

Mme. Jacques's Revenge

In the little town of San Morlaye, north of Paris, there lived a Spanish woman who was married to Henri Jacques, a French racetrack employee at nearby Chantilly. Soon after the Germans occupied the area they seized Henri Jacques and the Jacqueses' only son, Jules, and put them in a labor battalion for work on the Channel fortifications. Mme. Jacques's reaction was seemingly nonviolent, and she took to inviting several of the local German officers into her home for meals several evenings a week.

After one such evening the officers did not return to their quarters. The next day an orderly came looking for them and found them dead in the Jacqueses' kitchen. They had been drugged and their throats cut. Mme. Jacques was nowhere to be found. She had been smuggled back to her native Spain. After the war she returned to San Morlaye, but her husband and son had died in Germany, where they had been shipped by the Germans when work on the Channel fortifications was finished.

Mme. Jacques had accomplished her act of ret-

ribution by working with a small network of resistants that had already spontaneously sprung up in
the Chantilly-Senlis-San Morlaye area. One
member of this early resistance cell was the druggist in San Morlaye who had given Mme. Jacques
the drug used on the German officers. He was
later questioned by the German secret police but
insisted he had given the drug to Mme. Jacques as
sleeping medicine for her own use. His records
backed up his story, so he was allowed to go free,
but was placed under permanent surveillance. Despite this surveillance, the druggist continued his
resistance work.

Mme. Jacques was smuggled out of France by a
network of underground resistance families that
had sprung into existence to aid downed Allied
fliers escape from France.

The head of the underground network in this
area was another woman, a Mme. Lauro, a
French woman married to an Italian employee at
the Chantilly racetrack. Mme. Lauro worked all
through the war as an underground agent, using
her home as a safe house for downed airmen on
their way into Spain and actively harassing the
German garrison at Chantilly. One of the ways she
plagued the Germans was by obtaining hydro-
chloric acid and nitric acid from the druggist at
San Morlaye and pouring it onto food supplies in

the freight trains in the Chantilly railroad yards. She worked alone at this and at night, and somehow managed never to get caught.

When the British realized that underground networks such as the one north of Paris were springing up all over France, they made every effort to organize them. Trained British saboteurs were parachuted into France or landed along the coast at night to contact members of the French underground.

One of the first of these early networks to be aided by the British was at Vichy, capital of unoccupied France. It was to become one of the most famous of all the resistance organizations. Originally formed by Georges Loustanau-Laucau and a handful of his friends, this espionage network was called the Alliance. Gradually it grew to several thousand members, and its operation was taken over by Marie-Madeleine Fourcade, who became the only woman to lead a major French resistance organization. Under Marie-Madeleine the Alliance soon gained fame as far away as Berlin as "Noah's Ark." This was because Marie-Madeleine gave all of the key members of her underground network animals' names as their code names. Her own was Hedgehog.

With the launching of Noah's Ark, organized resistance against the German enemy in France truly became underground warfare.

II

The Most
Famous Network of
All

WHEN THE GERMANS occupied northern France in 1940, Marie-Madeleine Fourcade was a young Paris housewife. She was thirty, the mother of two children and separated from her husband. For several years she had worked as the executive secretary for a publishing house headed by Georges Loustanau-Laucau. Loustanau-Laucau was a veteran and hero of World War I, and since then had done secret-service work for the French government. His code name was Navarre.

Just before World War II began, Navarre had obtained the German Order of Battle from secret intelligence sources within Germany. It gave the troop disposition of all of Hitler's air, land, and sea forces and clearly indicated that Germany was about to strike. Impatient at the French government's refusal to act on this information and mistrusting a number of French officials, Navarre published the secret German Order of Battle in one of his magazines. Marie-Madeleine helped ready this material for publication.

For some months after World War II had begun, there was little fighting on land. During this so-called phony war Navarre continued to denounce the French military leaders for their refusal to act and was finally arrested and charged with anti-government activity. But when the Germans out-flanked the Maginot Line by invading the Low Countries — just as Navarre had predicted — he was released and given a military command. Before leaving for battle, Navarre advised Marie-Madeleine to leave Paris and join his wife and family at their country home in southern France in the Pyrénées. Navarre promised that when the collapse came he would join her and their other loyal friends there.

Shortly before Paris fell, Marie-Madeleine had sent her children to the safety of the island of

Noirmoutier in the Bay of Biscay, where they stayed with her mother. Soon afterward Marie-Madeleine and several friends headed south for the rendezvous with Navarre, but Navarre had been wounded in action and taken prisoner. When he partially recovered, however, he escaped from the German POW camp and headed for his Pyrénées home. He arrived there in late August. He found his family and friends waiting for him.

While she had been in the Pyrénées area waiting for Navarre, Marie-Madeleine had been aware that many French people had escaped through the mountains and into Spain. Some of them, she had heard, had even made their way from Spain to Gibraltar and thence to England to join de Gaulle's Free French. She assumed that when his wounds were fully healed this was what Navarre would want to do.

But Navarre would have none of that. He was filled with plans for establishing a resistance organization. After all, he pointed out, forty million French people could not simply abandon their homes and flee France, leaving their country in the hands of the Germans. He insisted they could most effectively fight the occupation by remaining in France and supplying the Free French and British with vital information about the enemy. Navarre had even made contact with certain agents through whom they could funnel this information to de Gaulle and British intelligence in London.

Navarre also thought they could operate most effectively out of Vichy. Marie-Madeleine was strongly opposed to having anything to do with what she regarded as traitors in that "phony capital."

But Navarre persisted, telling her she would have to learn how to deceive people. And where better to practice deception than in the heartland of the collaborationists?

Birth of Hedgehog

So it was decided to begin their resistance activities in Vichy. Navarre even had a name for his proposed organization. It was to be called the Crusade, and its members would be known as Crusaders. Within a few months the Crusade became the Alliance, and then about a year later, under Marie-Madeleine, was nicknamed Noah's Ark. She first decided upon animal code names for her agents when the Germans began to hunt them down like animals. Then it occurred to her that if the biblical flood could not destroy Noah's Ark and its precious cargo, the catastrophe of the German occupation would not be able to destroy her and the precious cargo in her "Ark." She thought of herself as a hedgehog (porcupine) with bristling quills warding off the enemy, so she took that animal as her own code name.

Marie-Madeleine did not have the least intention of becoming a resistance leader. But Navarre pointed out that he would have to lie low for fear of being recaptured, and it would be up to Marie-Madeleine to take charge of clandestine operations.

She objected, however, on the grounds that she was only a woman who had just turned thirty and that no one would take orders from her. Being a woman was her biggest advantage, Navarre said. Nobody would suspect a woman.

Marie-Madeleine still refused. She was a follower, not a leader. She wanted to take orders, not give them. She had assumed she would be taking orders from Navarre. But Navarre pointed out that he would be busy secretly organizing guerrillas for actual combat against the enemy. He would do the aboveground work; she would handle the underground.

Marie-Madeleine stubbornly insisted that she should be serving in the ranks, not directing others. If Navarre would not be the leader himself, he should pick someone else, not her. But there was no one else Navarre could fully trust.

So in the end Marie-Madeleine accepted, promising she would try not to disappoint him.

Actually, for several months, Navarre and Marie-Madeleine worked closely together. He furnished the ideas for forming resistance "patrols," as they called each underground cell, and she put the ideas into practice. They got full cooperation from British intelligence. In the swift downfall of France and the Dunkirk debacle, the British intelligence network on the continent had been all but destroyed. London's Special Operations Executive (SOE), which was established by Prime Minister Churchill in the summer of 1940 to wage clandestine warfare on the continent, was delighted to learn that a resistance organization had been formed at Vichy.

One of the first needs of any resistance group is radios. These the British supplied by secret airdrops. Once she had shortwave radios, Marie-Madeleine discovered it was relatively easy to recruit French former military radio operators who were itching to get back into action. Radio operators frequently recommended other friends, and soon a resistance cell would be formed. Actually she had little trouble obtaining recruits with many varied talents. The whole of unoccupied France seemed filled with young men and women who were eager to come aboard her resistance ark, not merely two-by-two but in tens and twenties. Navarre cautioned her against accepting potential agents too hastily, for fear she might take aboard a member of the German intelligence, or Abwehr, in disguise.

Recruiting Agents

From among these early recruits Marie-Madeleine selected those she thought best suited and situated to obtain vital intelligence information, such as German troop dispositions, the location of gasoline storage dumps, the location of German airfields, and the number of aircraft ready for action. It was also important to know the number of submarines and merchant ships entering French ports along the west coast and in the Mediterranean. This called for cells at Saint-Nazaire, Marseilles, and Nice. The British were also keenly interested in the bombing results of their air raids on German targets in France.

Navarre also advised Marie-Madeleine to be on the lookout for expert forgers among her recruits. These were needed to make false papers and identification documents for resistance members moving into and out of the occupied zone. Some of these forgers were recruited directly from the crime underworld of the major cities. Others were men who had worked as legitimate engravers but were now willing to turn their hand to outwitting the Germans. Eventually British intelligence supplied her with all of the forged documents she needed, but in the beginning she had to obtain them herself.

Code Name: Shrimp

Occasionally Marie-Madeleine was surprised by having information appear virtually out of the blue by an agent she had not even recruited. This was the case with a teenage girl who later was given the code name of Shrimp. Shrimp repaired fishermen's nets in a little shop at Brest, whose harbor was taken over as a German submarine base. German submariners got into the habit of bringing their new life jackets to Shrimp for fitting and their old life jackets for repairs. While chatting with her customers, Shrimp was able to learn the number of the U-boat on which each of them served. So when there was a sudden rush by a certain U-boat crew to obtain their jackets, she knew that submarine was going out on patrol. Shrimp was eager to pass this information on to a resistance member who could make use of it; she finally encountered a member of the Ark called Unicorn. Unicorn was somewhat suspicious of having such valuable intelligence fall into his lap, but took the risk of having it radioed to London. British Royal Navy bombers immediately reacted and gained the first of many submarine "kills" as a result of Shrimp's efforts.

In her autobiography Marie-Madeleine later told how she spent most of her early days as a resistance leader. Her activities included selecting recruits, obtaining radios and deciding where they were to go, establishing secure letterboxes or "drops," where agents could deposit information and other agents could pick it up, devising and assigning code names, learning and teaching message codes—codes were usually supplied by the British—and double-checking all information. She also was responsible for the millions of francs for the resistance fighters the British supplied in addition to radios. This money arrived in airdrops or was sent by couriers.

The Ideal Spy Cell

As intelligence agents before her had learned, the largely self-taught Marie-Madeleine soon discovered that the ideal intelligence cell should consist of a source, that is, someone who obtains the information; a letterbox or drop where the information is deposited and collected; a courier who picks up and delivers the information; a central agent who receives the report; and a radio operator to relay the information to intelligence headquarters. At headquarters there is a person called a control who is in charge of or "runs" central agents in the field. Letterboxes or drops were not necessarily in post offices, although these were sometimes used. Usually a drop was at the home of a resistance member or at some other prearranged location.

That there was great danger inherent in all of her early resistance activities Marie-Madeleine had no doubt. But for the most part she was far too busy to spend much time worrying about the fact that she was risking her life. Now and again, however, one of her resistance patrols would simply disappear and afterward she would learn that its members had been apprehended, tortured, and shot.

Although most resistance members would eventually crack under the torments of German torture if they were captured, and divulge whatever information they had, not many had much information to give. This was because Marie-Madeleine had learned from Navarre that only one member of each cell should know the code name of just one other member of another cell. In this way, it was hoped, the destruction of one cell would be limited to just that one cell and the capture of one or all of its members would not result in uncovering the entire resistance network. In actual practice there was no wholly foolproof way of preventing a cell's being penetrated. In addition, of course, code names were always used, so few members knew who their fellow resistants were. Most resistants wanted to know as little as possible about anyone else in their cell, so if they were caught they would have little information to give. Thus when a recruit began asking too many questions he or she immediately came under suspicion.

By 1941 Marie-Madeleine had spread her network from Vichy to Saint-Nazaire, Marseilles, Nice, Brest, Pau, Lyons, and finally into Paris itself. Each "patrol" had its own radio transmitter, and there was a regular courier service into Madrid and the British embassy there. At least weekly, and frequently several times a week, vital intelligence information would be sent and received via these sending and receiving stations. This information was not merely what the resistance agents had managed to pick up, but more and more regularly was also answers to questions sent to them by the SOE in London. Such SOE queries often included requests for the names of new German army commanders in certain areas, troop strength and morale, civilian morale, and, as always, up-to-date information on the enemy Order of Battle.

Early in 1941 Marie-Madeleine passed on to London some intelligence that the British evidently did not believe. At least they did not act on it. (The resistance was not supposed to evaluate information, only gather it.) This information was supplied by Maurice Coustenoble (Tiger), who had picked it up from the Paris network. A reliable informant there said that Germany was about to break its neutrality pact with the Soviet Union and invade that country. Later it was learned that the Communist resistance movement in Paris also passed this word to Moscow, but Premier Joseph Stalin refused to believe it. Germany did invade on June 11, and the Soviet Union then became a member of the Allies.

By late 1941 Marie-Madeleine and her resistance organization had also become skilled at setting up various fronts to hide their activities. Perhaps their most successful one was a wholesale vegetable business that one of the agents, Gabriel Rivière (Wolf), managed at Marseilles. Rivière bought the business for 40,000 francs supplied by the British. It was money well invested because the warehouse was ideal as a storage place for resistance radio equipment and other supplies. In addition it served as an excellent meeting place, since resistance members could mingle with the numerous workers and business people who were constantly coming and going. Also, resistance agents traveling in other parts of France could claim a connection with the Marseilles vegetable market operation if they were picked up and questioned by the Germans.

Rivière's wife, Madeleine, and one of his partners actually worked in the shop taking care of the daily trade while Rivière himself went about *his* business of obtaining intelligence information about German shipping activities in the Mediterranean. Ironically, the Rivière wholesale vegetable enterprise proved to be a financially successful business in its own right throughout the war.

A Traitor Is Unmasked

Unfortunately, not all of the assistance provided the Navarre–Marie-Madeleine resistance network by the British was equally successful. In 1942 when the network was expanding its operations the British sent one of their agents to join them. Named Blanchet, he was known at the time only by the code name Bla. Bla was dropped into France by parachute, and the day after he landed he suffered an attack of appendicitis. He was safely hidden at resistance headquarters in Pau, and Marie-Madeleine helped nurse him back to health.

Soon after his recovery Bla began acting suspiciously and seemed abnormally interested in obtaining from Marie-Madeleine all of the details of her resistance organization. She told him as little as possible and queried the British about their agent. They vouched for Bla's legitimacy.

Once he was in the field as an operative agent, calamities seemed to follow in his wake. Here and there a patrol would be visited by Bla and a short time after his departure the patrol's members would be picked up by the Germans. When Marie-Madeleine's own most trusted aides began voicing their suspicions of Bla, she again reported her misgivings to the British in London. After a longer than usual delay, the startling reply came back that Marie-Madeleine was indeed correct: Bla, the British had belatedly discovered, was a traitor working for the German Gestapo. He had apparently infiltrated British intelligence as a member of Sir Oswald Mosley's fascist organization, which had been active in England before the war. The message also authorized Bla's execution.

In carrying out the execution order things also went wrong. Marie-Madeleine had obtained a number of poison tablets. These were usually carried by agents who intended to use them to commit suicide if they were captured and feared they might break down and talk. One of these tablets was administered to Bla in a bowl of hot soup. He suffered only a few stomach cramps. Another tablet was given him in a cup of hot tea. Still there were no results.

At this point a more experienced agent known as Eagle (Léon Faye, who later became the military head of the network) arrived on the scene. He asked how the pills had been administered. When told, he said the pills should not have been put into any hot liquid because that diluted their effectiveness.

Eagle then took charge of the execution. How it was carried out Marie-Madeleine never knew. She left Bla with several of her most trusted aides and the next day was told the deed had been done. But in a final gallant gesture, perhaps in repayment for her earlier role as his nurse, Bla had sent her a message: she must move the resistance headquarters from Vichy because the Germans were going to take over all of unoccupied France on November 11.

The Invasion of North Africa

Bla's final warning proved true. The United States was now in the war, and the first joint

Anglo-American land operation was the invasion of North Africa. It took place on November 8, 1942. Its purpose was to take over all of the former French bases in North Africa and to drive out the Germans there under General Erwin Rommel. Once this was accomplished the Allies would control the Mediterranean and an attack could then be launched on southern France and against Italy. The Germans knew they must now have direct access to all of southern France not only to prepare for such an Allied assault but also to supply their armies in North Africa. As Bla had predicted, Vichy was occupied by the Germans on November 11.

Months before the Allied invasion of North Africa, Navarre had gone there to try and stir up a revolt among some of Marshal Pétain's collaborationist officers stationed in Algiers. The plot had been discovered and Navarre arrested. Again he managed to escape from jail and returned to France. He was now a marked man, and Marie-Madeleine urged him to flee to London. But Navarre insisted upon fighting on in France, especially since it enabled him to be near his family. Again he was arrested and this time sentenced to a long jail term. When the Germans occupied all of France, Navarre was removed to a prison in Germany where he would be out of reach of any possible rescue attempts by his resistance friends.

Marie-Madeleine was now left to carry on alone. She was quick to realize that with the Allies now in North Africa it was more important than ever to maintain a resistance network in southern France. Vital information could be obtained and given to the Allies not only about German troop movements in southern France but also concerning when and how many aircraft were taking off from southern France's Luftwaffe air fields.

Marie-Madeleine moved out of Vichy and established mobile headquarters at Marseilles, Bordeaux, Nice, Pau, and in any other sizable city where detection seemed least likely and valuable intelligence information was readily available.

Hedgehog's Trip in a Mailbag

As the person now in complete charge of the Noah's Ark network, Marie-Madeleine was requested to meet with a British intelligence representative in Madrid. This she agreed to do—but how to make the journey became a problem. Jean Boutron (Bull), a network aide at the French embassy in Vichy provided the means. (The Germans still allowed the French to maintain a puppet government there.) At least once a week, and often more frequently, diplomatic mailbags were sent from Vichy to the Spanish capital. Because they were officially sealed none of these mailbags was allowed to be opened by border guards. The aide's suggestion: Marie-Madeleine was to be put into one of these diplomatic mailbags and transported to Spain via the railroad that ran through the Pyrénées.

Although she had slimmed down considerably under a wartime diet, Marie-Madeleine was not a small woman. At five feet six inches she had more than a little difficulty fitting into a mailbag four feet by two feet. Nevertheless, she managed the feat, and the bag containing the curled-up Hedgehog was placed in the backseat of Boutron's Citroen automobile. The Citroen in turn was placed on a railroad flatcar, and the journey to Madrid began.

Partially to disguise the mailbag Boutron had thrown several automobile tires onto the car's backseat. En route, these tires slid off the seat and onto the bag containing Marie-Madeleine. To make matters worse there were many delays, and the journey took nine interminable hours. At some stops Boutron was able to leave the passenger compartment of the train and come back and open the mailbag so Marie-Madeleine could breathe more freely and stretch her paralyzed limbs. But these were her only respites.

In addition, the journey through the high Pyrénées at night was a frigidly cold one. Mercifully the cold and her incredibly cramped position made Marie-Madeleine lose consciousness during the final hours of her ordeal.

Once across the Pyrénées and into Spain, the car and its valuable mailbag were removed from the train and Boutron then drove it on to Madrid. By the time they arrived, Marie-Madeleine had been released from her mailbag prison and revived with hot food and wine. When they reached Madrid she seemed none the worse for wear—until she realized that she must make the return journey in the same fashion.

The main reason British intelligence wanted to see and talk with Marie-Madeleine was that for a long time they had not known that Hedgehog was a woman. Now they needed to decide whether she was capable of handling the top job. They had not talked long with Marie-Madeleine before they were convinced that she was ideally suited for her role. They supplied her with new codes to pass on to her radio operators. They also gave her a supply of newly developed invisible ink with which to write code messages to be carried by courier. They promised her an airdrop of new and more compact radio transmitters, cautioning her against letting any of her operators send messages for longer than a few moments at a time and warning her about staying in one place for longer than twenty minutes after transmitting. German detection devices had been steadily improving, and they could now zero in on an operating transmitter with incredible speed.

After several days of consultation with the British in Madrid it was finally time for Marie-Madeleine to start her return journey. She looked forward to it with great dread, but this time it was not nearly so much of an ordeal. There were fewer delays. Within several hours she was back in France and released once again. She was driven from the train in Boutron's Citroen and deposited safely at Pau. Safely for the time being, that is. Within a matter of months Marie-Madeleine would be fleeing for her life and her Noah's Ark would be threatened with foundering. And not only her network would be endangered. Several other resistance organizations that by now had grown even larger than Noah's Ark would also be threatened with destruction. During the terrible year of 1943 the whole French resistance movement would lose almost two-thirds of its members.

III

Jean Moulin's Tragic Story

WHILE NOAH'S ARK was being launched, several other major resistance networks were also established elsewhere in France.

Noah's Ark was a unique organization whose very nature, its leaders felt, might be destroyed by involvement with other, more ordinary groups. This was also the attitude of the staff of the Museum of Man in Paris led by Boris Vildé, as well as that of Gilbert Renault (Colonel Rémy), whose organization, the Confrérie de Notre Dame, supplied the British with Hitler's plans for the Atlantic Wall.

The leader of another relatively small resistance

network known as Franc-Tireur, Jean-Pierre Levy, perhaps expressed the desire for independence best. The larger an organization became, he said, the easier it would be for it to be infiltrated by the enemy. He also said he feared that jealousy and rivalry among a large organization's leaders would lead to the organization's destruction.

Communist Resistants

One major resistance organization that remained especially independent throughout most of the war was made up of French Communists. And for the most part the other French resistance groups were more than content to keep the Communists out of their affairs. In the beginning, of course, while the Soviet-German neutrality pact was in effect the French Communists flatly refused to resist the German occupation of France. When Hitler broke this pact by invading the Soviet Union, the French Communists immediately became active in the underground movement—but they continued to guard their independence. Their reason for doing so was clear enough: once the Germans were defeated and driven out of France, the Communists were determined to establish their own form of government in France with direct allegiance to the Soviet Union.

Communist-resistance activity frequently took the form of assassination of German occupation troops. This activity was a two-edged sword, because it resulted in savage retaliation by the Germans. When a Communist killed a German field commander at Nantes, for example, in October of 1941, fifty Frenchmen were taken as hostages and shot. This did not stop the assassinations, nor did the assassinations stop the reprisals.

The Maquis

Another resistance group, or combination of groups actually, that was highly independent by the very nature and background of its members, was the so-called Maquis. The Maquis was active mainly in rural, and especially mountainous, areas. Its members took their name from bushes which grew along country roads that were known as *maquis*.

Despite this widespread and stubborn desire for independence among all of the resistance networks, it was believed by both the British Special Operations Executive (SOE) and Free France's General Charles de Gaulle in London that these networks must be unified in order for them to be most effective. A leading French resistance fighter who fully agreed with the SOE and de Gaulle was a man who was to become one of the great underground heroes. His name was Jean Moulin.

In the beginning General de Gaulle was not wholly convinced that the resistance could play a major role in the liberation of France. He thought of it mainly as a morale factor in keeping the spirit of freedom alive. Liberation, de Gaulle was convinced, would have to be brought about by an invading Allied army. But when Jean Moulin and others suggested to de Gaulle that an invading army's chances of success would be greatly increased if it could link up with a unified resistance army, he was quick to see the possibilities of such a plan. This was the birth of the idea of the French Forces of the Interior (FFI). From idea to realization, however, was something else again.

First of all, de Gaulle gave Moulin written authority to head a newly established Conseil National de la Résistance. Theoretically this National Resistance Council was to have complete control over all of the French resistance networks. But at first it did not quite work out that way. For one thing, Moulin and Combat's Henri Frenay violently disagreed with each other about resistance policies, and there were frequent disagreements among other underground leaders as well. Nevertheless, Moulin valiantly continued the struggle for a unified resistance, a struggle that would end in success—but not before Moulin's torture and death at the hands of the Nazis.

Moulin's Struggle for Unification

Since its revolution, France, which is somewhat smaller than Texas, has been divided for purposes of governmental administration into some ninety departments. On a map these departments look somewhat like American counties, but their importance has always been more nearly the equivalent of that of American states. Each of these departments is headed by a prefect, a top administrative official appointed by the nation's central government. One of these prefects in 1940 was Jean Moulin. He headed the department of Eure-et-Loire and, at forty, was the youngest prefect in France.

When the Germans occupied most of France, many government officials fled into the unoccupied zone. Most of those few who remained behind collaborated with the Germans. Moulin neither fled nor became a collaborator. Since he was such an important and highly regarded official, the Germans decided to try and break him. When Moulin refused to sign a statement saying that the murder of certain French civilians had been committed by French soldiers rather than by the actual murderers, the Nazis, the Germans beat him and threw him into jail. There he was further brutalized until he lost consciousness.

When Moulin came to he found himself in a cell with a female corpse. Also in the cell were some pieces of glass from a broken window. Afraid that if he had to undergo any further torture he might weaken and sign whatever statement the Germans asked him to sign, Moulin decided to commit suicide. He cut his throat with one of the pieces of glass and slowly began to bleed to death. But when his guards found him he was still alive. They rushed him to a hospital, where he gradually recovered. Upon his recovery he was released from the hospital only to find that the French collaborationist government had dismissed him from the civil service. Moulin soon decided to join the French resistance movement, which was just beginning to become active.

For many months he traveled secretly throughout France, working with the various resistance groups. One of the reasons he kept on the move was because he was well known to both French collaborationist officials and the German intelligence, or Abwehr, agents. In his travels among the various resistance networks he became convinced that if they were all joined into one master network they could cooperate more efficiently with British intelligence and General de Gaulle. When he talked with the network leaders, they apparently agreed with him—mainly because they badly needed the money and supplies essential to their resistance activities, paramilitary matériel that was only available in large quantities from the British.

Moulin decided to go to London himself and contact the SOE and de Gaulle. He was smuggled out of France to Lisbon, Portugal, where he was interviewed by the SOE and then sent on to London, where he was turned over to de Gaulle.

Moulin was able to give de Gaulle a detailed report of the state of resistance efforts in France, and the general was impressed with the extent of the underground activities. He was also impressed with Moulin's vision of a unified resistance movement. After several weeks of discussion and planning, Moulin prepared to return to France with his written authority from de Gaulle to proceed with the unification effort.

Soon after Moulin was parachuted back into France in January of 1942, he contacted Frenay, the head of Combat, and d'Astier, the head of Libération, both of whom pledged allegiance to the plan. They both expressed misgivings about "taking orders from London," but the promise of supplies and money in sizable quantities decided them in favor of unification. Moulin then went on to contact the leaders of Franc-Tireur, Noah's Ark, and other resistance groups, all of whom gave him at least qualified approval.

Unification plans continued to go well until Moulin began to press the network leaders into forming a regular military organization that could go into open combat against the Germans. This had been somewhat similar to the plan Navarre of Noah's Ark once had formulated, but Navarre was now in jail. Frenay was all in favor of anything that smacked of the military and said he would agree to the formation of such an underground army—provided he were named its commander in chief. D'Astier and Levy, head of Franc-Tireur, flatly opposed the idea and began to mount efforts to oust Moulin from his overall leadership role as de Gaulle's chief emissary in France. The various Maquis leaders and their organizations had been actively and successfully waging guerrilla warfare for months against the Germans, and they were not about to join anybody's army.

Moulin's purpose in forming this underground army was to have it ready to rise in revolt against the German occupation forces when the Allies invaded France. He still thought this plan was essential; and so did de Gaulle, who hoped one day to march behind such an army into Paris and become the first president of a liberated France. But temporarily, at least, the only resistance fighters who seemed to agree with Moulin were the Communists. However, their army, if one were formed, would not offer allegiance to de Gaulle. It would, in fact, oppose him and install a Communist comrade as president once the Germans were driven out. What was more, they would not offer Moulin any assurance that they would wait for an Allied invasion to strike for control of the country. Already they claimed to be killing Germans at the rate of five or six hundred a month via the assassination route, and this was only one step short of open warfare. Open warfare would bring instant and massive retaliation by the Germans and the poorly equipped resistance would be destroyed.

As a result of this disagreement Moulin temporarily backed away from his underground army plans. Instead he pushed for a general meeting of resistance leaders at which a formal declaration of unity would be made. This meeting was held in the spring of 1943 in a secure apartment in Paris. This was the first actual meeting of the National Resistance Council. It was attended by sixteen of the top resistance leaders. When it began there was much suspicion and disagreement among the rival representatives. But when it ended after several days, much of the suspicion and jealousy had been dissipated by Jean Moulin's persuasive words and the noble challenge he presented. He spoke to the leaders of the vision of a unified France that could be made possible by a unified resistance. He told them of de Gaulle's dream of a free and democratic country that could be born out of their sacrifice. In the end they swore a solemn oath of allegiance not only to unification of their resistance efforts but also to de Gaulle.

At the end of June, several weeks after the Paris meeting, Jean Moulin was picked up by the Gestapo.

Moulin Is Betrayed

Moulin's betrayal was just one of dozens that virtually destroyed several of the French resistance networks in 1943. It began at Marseilles when Jean Multon, a top Combat agent, was arrested by the Abwehr. To avoid being tortured, Multon agreed to go to work for the Gestapo. Within a matter of days Multon led his captors to more than a hundred resistance members in Marseilles. He then traveled with the Gestapo to Lyons, where scores of other resistants were betrayed. Frantically, Frenay broadcast a "kill" order on Multon, but it was too late. The effects of Multon's betrayals began to snowball. Here and there another captured resistant also broke under torture and led the Gestapo to the meeting places of his or her resistance comrades. The destruction of the networks began to reach the proportions of a massacre.

Eventually the series of betrayals reached so many of the underground cells and caused such panic that Moulin requested aid from London. The British parachuted into France several agents to help him rebuild the networks, but these agents themselves soon were threatened with capture and had to go into hiding.

Moulin was captured on June 21, 1943, at what was believed to be a safe house just outside Lyons in the suburb of Caluire. He was attending a meeting held to reestablish some order out of the chaos caused by the mass arrests. The safe house, however, had been under observation for days by a Gestapo Chief, Klaus Barbie, and his men, who had been alerted to the meeting by one of the resistance defectors. Shortly after Moulin arrived, Gestapo Chief Barbie and his agents burst through the doors of the house and arrested all present.

Moulin was thrown into Lyons Prison, where he was tortured for days. Such torture usually began with severe beatings. Then a prisoner's fingers might be broken one at a time or all at once by placing his or her hand in the space between an open door and the doorway frame and then closing the door. If this produced no positive results, the prisoner was subjected to near drownings in a bathtub, followed by resuscitation—a process that would sometimes be repeated numerous times. As the war progressed, the Gestapo became increasingly skilled at the near drowning of prisoners. These near drownings might be followed or alternated with electric shocks. This was done by attaching electrodes to particularly sensitive areas of the prisoner's body. Few prisoners could withstand such tortures.

Moulin was seen by another arrested resistance member in the Lyons prison on June 24. This man was Christian Pineau, who found an unconscious man lying in the prison exercise yard. Moulin had been so badly beaten that Pineau at first failed to recognize him. When he did, he managed to force a few drops of water past Moulin's disfigured lips. Moulin regained consciousness for a few moments but was unable to speak.

Later Moulin was sent by train to Germany. Somewhere on that railway journey he died. But never during the course of his ordeal did he divulge any of his vast store of knowledge about the resistance which he helped to unify. As word of

Moulin's death spread, the manner of his dying served to inspire further those resistance members who were left to regroup and rebuild the devastated resistance movement into an even more powerful and unified organization than it had been before.

Hedgehog Escapes to England

One of those who had narrowly escaped being caught in the Gestapo's dragnet raids was Noah's Ark's Hedgehog, Marie-Madeleine. She managed to elude capture, but dozens of her agents were seized at Ussel, Paris, Toulouse, Marseilles, Pau, Nice, and Lyons. She radioed a coded message to London informing officials there of the disaster, and the SOE ordered her to leave France. At first Marie-Madeleine refused to go. London pointed out that she could probably do more good in London by way of laying plans to rebuild her network, and she certainly could do no good if she were captured. Finally, in mid-July, she agreed to get out.

On July 18, 1943, Marie-Madeleine was flown out of France after making rendezvous with a Lysander plane in a farm field in a rural area outside Paris. When she arrived in London one of the senior staff officers of the SOE told her he regarded her being there as nothing short of a miracle.

Why? Marie-Madeleine wanted to know.

Because, he pointed out, the average life of a resistance leader in the field was six months. And Marie-Madeleine had been at it for two and a half years.

Marie-Madeleine, who was guilt-ridden at having left her comrades behind, told the SOE officer that she was already making plans to return. This was a vow that she would keep—but this time she too would be captured by the Gestapo. Meanwhile, Marie-Madeleine went to work for the SOE in London.

IV

Secret Agent Operations

THE BRITISH HAD great success with their overall intelligence operations since the start of the war. The most outstanding of these successes was classified not merely Top Secret but Ultra Secret, or simply Ultra. It involved the capture of a German electric coding machine the British called Enigma. Enigma had been perfected by the Germans before the war.

The Ultra Secret: Enigma

Somewhat like a modern computer, Enigma could be programmed to encode messages into almost limitless variations — as many as one hundred and fifty million million million, according to historian John Keegan. This programming could also be and frequently was changed as often as every twenty-four hours. Messages in plain text that were then encoded by Enigma could only be decoded if one also had an Enigma machine and knew how its programming worked.

In 1939 the Poles had captured an Enigma machine and turned a model of it over to the British. British scientists located at Bletchley had then constructed their own Enigma and solved its secrets. As a result, all during the war British intelligence could decode German Top Secret military messages soon after they were encoded and sent.

Information gained from Ultra intercepts had to be used with great caution, of course, since if it were passed out too freely the Germans would soon realize the riddle of their electronic code machine had been solved. They then would revert to old-fashioned coded messages using new codes which would take much time and painstaking effort to crack and decode.

Interestingly, Enigma had a keyboard that looked much like a typewriter. Inadvertently, the Germans had allowed at least one picture to be taken of an Enigma operator at work. It showed

General Heinze Guderian in his command car with his Enigma operator at his side. When this picture appeared in the foreign press, the operator was simply assumed to be a clerk typist.

Top Allied commanders were all supplied with carefully monitored Ultra intelligence. After the war when the Ultra story was finally told by Bletchley's F.W. Winterbottom, several Allied commanders were asked why they hadn't defeated the Germans more easily when they knew the enemy's intentions even before various battles began. The answer was simply that the commanders thought such intelligence was too good to be true. If they acted on it and it was wrong, *they* would be blamed for failure, not their intelligence sources.

Double Agents

British intelligence had also been highly successful in turning German agents into double agents or reluctant allies of the British secret service. This was called the Double-Cross System, and its mastermind was Sir John Masterman. Because Great Britain was an island nation, once an enemy agent was parachuted or put ashore he or she had little chance of returning to the Continent. As soon as a German agent in Great Britain began to send out radio messages, it was usually only a matter of time before the agent was captured.

Captured German agents had just two chances: slim and none. They could become double agents, working for the British but still pretending to be German spies, or they could be executed. Most chose to become double agents. As the number of double agents working in Great Britain increased, it became easier to pick up newly infiltrated German spies, since their arrival was almost immediately known by their double-agent colleagues.

The Double-Cross System also had to be handled with great care so that German intelligence would not realize their spy system in Great Britain had beem compromised. Consequently, German agents who became British double agents were fed a diet of carefully prepared—and harmless—intelligence information that they would relay to German intelligence headquarters.

Triple Agent: The Cat

Very occasionally there were instances of spies becoming so-called triple agents. One such complex creature was a French woman, Mathilde Carré, who was known as La Chatte (The Cat). While she was establishing Noah's Ark, Marie-Madeleine had heard of The Cat, but security reports about her questioned her loyalty. Consequently, despite her apt Noah's Ark–type name, The Cat was never recruited by Marie-Madeleine. These suspicions proved to be well founded.

Mathilde Carré was a very attractive woman in her thirties who joined the resistance movement against the Germans in Paris early in the war. The small unit to which she belonged was called Interallié and was one of the first to establish contact with British intelligence. She soon became one of Interallié's most effective members and was nicknamed The Cat by her resistance comrades.

Interallié had not been in operation very long, however, before it was penetrated by Abwehr agents. Among those picked up was The Cat, although she later claimed to a British agent, Pierre de Vomécourt, that she had evaded capture. De Vomécourt was a native Frenchman but had been recruited as a British agent in 1939. He was also active in the resistance.

The Cat had only been in German captivity for a few hours, but during that time she was persuaded to become a double agent working for the Germans. She promptly proved her new loyalty by leading the Abwehr to the safe houses and meeting places of those Interallié members who had eluded capture. One of those she betrayed was her sweetheart, Claude Jouffert, whom she identified in a cafe by kissing him fondly.

The Cat, with Abwehr agents looking over her shoulder, soon resumed contact with British intelligence by radio. But the brief delay in the transmission of messages from Interallié had aroused British suspicions. De Vomécourt was told to test The Cat.

De Vomécourt's test was simple enough. He merely asked The Cat if she could secure some important official enemy documents. Within a matter of hours The Cat handed the documents to de Vomécourt. Such impossibly prompt action confirmed de Vomécourt's suspicion. He told her he was going to shoot her as a German spy. The Cat pleaded for mercy, and de Vomécourt relented to the point of asking her if she was willing to once again go to work for France and the British. The Cat readily agreed to become a triple agent.

But that was as far as her turncoat career went. She was soon smuggled out of France and turned over to British intelligence interrogators in London. The Cat readily told them everything she knew, believing she was now in the hands of sympathetic compatriots. But when she finally finished talking, the British threw her in jail, where she remained until the end of the war. After the war she was returned to France and tried for treason. At first she was sentenced to death for betraying her Interallié comrades, but this sentence was later commuted to life imprisonment. In 1954 she was pardoned.

When the Abwehr learned of de Vomécourt's role in recruiting The Cat, it took out its revenge on him for The Cat's betrayal. He was tracked down, arrested, and thrown into Fresnes prison, where he was tortured unmercifully. But de Vomécourt never uttered a word and was finally shipped to a prison in Germany. He survived the war and was a witness at The Cat's trial.

Not all of the many Allied agents who aided the French resistance were so conveniently available as de Vomécourt. A few were recruited from among the Free French, but most had to be recruited and trained outside the French community.

Agent Casualties

By the middle of the war several hundred British agents and an equal number of American agents had been parachuted into France. They were greatly outnumbered by the several thousand German counterintelligence agents whose job it was to track them down. Of some 393

British spies sent into France up to this time, 110 were arrested and shot or deported to Germany. Only a handful survived. American intelligence never issued actual casualty figures, but they were equally high.

At the beginning of the war cooperation between American and British agents in the field was sadly lacking. Later in the war when cooperation among the various Allied intelligence agencies finally made working together in the field feasible, so-called Jedburgh teams of agents were formed. These three-man teams consisted of an American, a Frenchman, and a Briton plus occasionally a radio operator. Jedburgh, or Jed, teams were code-named by the SOE after the area in England where they were trained. Their purpose was to join the resistance after the Allied landings and act as liaison between resistance networks and advancing Allied troops. Jed team members wore regular army uniforms to prevent their being shot as spies if they were captured by the Germans.

To form these Jed teams fifty French-speaking men were recruited from the American army and fifty from the British army, and fifty English-speaking men were recruited from the Free French soldiers who had fled France and were in North Africa. They were given paratrooper and guerrilla warfare training in the British Midlands.

The main problem with the Jed teams turned out to be disagreement over which man, if any, of the bilingual trio was to be in charge. Each country's team member proved to be fiercely nationalistic and insisted on being the leader. Since leadership by committee would not work in a combat situation, a leader had to be appointed by higher military authority—a decision that did little to eliminate the rivalry among the three-man teams.

This command confusion was compounded during the Allied invasion of southern France when seven Jed teams were parachuted in to coordinate resistance efforts several days before the Allied landings. First of all, several separate resistance networks insisted that the Jed teams that had joined them were led by the highest-ranking officers, so their decisions should prevail over all the others. One resistance group even claimed that *their* Jed team had a general in charge—most Jed team members were lieutenants and captains— and refused orders from anyone else.

Nevertheless, despite this modest comedy of errors, the Jed teams did provide a definite amount of command control without which complete chaos could well have resulted when the Allies came ashore. One of the main problems was making certain that the Allies would recognize resistance bands as friendly and not assume they were the enemy and start shooting at them. Jed teams accompanied by resistance fighters were able to establish initial contact with the troops coming ashore and thus prevent this possibility from becoming a tragic reality.

Recruiting Agents

Regular British and American agents to be sent into France were recruited from the general population in Great Britain and the United States. No one ever figured out exactly what it took to make a good agent, so volunteers were recruited from all walks of life, all trades, and all professions. There were no specific requirements, although it helped if a prospect was bilingual. Fluent French-speaking candidates, however, were few and far between, so most recruits had to be taught the language through a process of total immersion—conversing in nothing but French twenty-four hours a day.

Spy Schools

Most Anglo-American spy candidates received their basic training at a camp in Canada. The

Canada site was chosen and set up in 1940 at the suggestion of the United States, which was not yet in the war. Advanced training was at first also in Canada but later at a camp in Fairfax, Virginia.

Canada also had another advantage as a location for the spy school, and that was its large French-speaking population. French Canadians, of course, speak the language somewhat differently from native French people, but the difference is not so great that it mattered for training purposes. The language that the candidates learned was authentic French. The French-Canadian environment and populace enabled the Allies to create an authentic French village and fill it with authentic French villagers, much like those the trainees would encounter in France. This Hollywood-like set with its well-trained cast of "extras" was complete, right down to German secret police posing as native French men and women. They delighted in encountering trainees and suddenly asking them questions in English. All too often the surprised trainees replied in their native tongue—a dead giveaway, of course, if the same situation occurred once the spies were actually in France.

Trainees were also "arrested," and their clothing checked for any telltale labels or English or American laundry or dry-cleaning marks. Authentic French clothing was appropriated from French refugees and issued to the spy trainees, but all too often this clothing was cleaned in American or Canadian laundries or cleaning establishments and bore their telltale marks.

Rugged physical training was a major part of the spy-school program. Agents in the field had to be prepared to undergo great physical as well as mental stress. Weapons training and the use of explosives were also part of the curriculum. After a day on the obstacle course, a trainee might be arrested and subjected to relentless interrogation by the school "Gestapo." These sessions were far from make-believe, trainees often being subjected to a certain amount of actual physical punishment.

No effort was spared at the spy school to break down prospective agents' ingrained habits and teach them how to blend in with the French populace. Americans did not have to learn to look to the left to check oncoming traffic before crossing a street, as did their British counterparts. (In Britain traffic moves on the left-hand side of the road; In France, as in the United States, it moves on the right.) French-Canadian drivers in the spy school seemed to take delight in trying to run down British spy trainees who looked the wrong way when they stepped off a curb. Americans did, however, have to learn such things as keeping their fork in their left hand while eating and not shift it back and forth from hand to hand. (Alert Gestapo agents would be quick to spot such incriminating mistakes.) Americans also had to break their habit of drinking water or milk at meals, rather than wine. Other rules of the road included not going bareheaded but wearing a beret; hands were to be kept out of one's pockets; one should not stride along athletically but slouch and shuffle; one should not whistle or sing—not only for fear of attracting attention but because an American or British tune might pop out.

Smoking materials were not infrequently used to trap trainees. A French-Canadian member of the spy-school cast of villagers might stop and chat with a trainee who was priding himself on his fluent French and secure in the knowledge that his clothing was authentic down to his shoestrings. Then the villager would apparently drop his villager's role, congratulate the trainee on his convincing masquerade efforts, and casually ask the trainee for a cigarette. Out would pop a pack of Lucky Strikes or Players and usually, in the case of Americans, a Zippo lighter. Such glaring blunders were finally eliminated when the French resistance smuggled out of France packs of Gauloise cigarettes as well as French matches, which were enormously difficult for resistance members to

obtain. Finally American and British intelligence
skilled at creating false identity papers also took
to manufacturing false French cigarette packages,
and French cigarettes were secretly manufactured
by an American tobacco company.

Military men who became agent trainees had
habits that had become ingrained while serving as
soldiers, sailors, or fliers. For one thing they were
cautioned against falling in step with one another
if they were walking with someone else, a military
man's common habit. In fact, group movement
was discouraged because this too attracted attention. Taught to respond instantly to commands,
ex-military men were also caught by these reflex
actions. One reflex action was to come to attention when a superior officer entered a room. Now
and again an American or British teacher would
don one of their country's officer's uniforms and,
accompanied by an aide, approach a group of spy
trainees. The aide would bark out, "ATTENSH-
hut!" and all too frequently several of the trainees
would pop to attention.

During the course of his training, each prospective agent was told to pick a cover name and de-
vise a cover story to use in France. Agents were
required to do this themselves so their new identities would become second nature to them. During staged interrogations these cover stories were

taken apart, from the trainee's birth to the present, and any mistakes or stumbling over the trainee's new autobiography instantly landed him in a jail cell. Here he might remain in solitary confinement and without food for twenty-four hours before being interrogated again. Some trainees lived and breathed their cover stories to the point where they virtually forgot their true identities.

Anglo-American Team

American agents were members of the Office of Strategic Services (OSS), which was headed by Major General William ''Wild Bill'' Donovan, a hero of World War I. Up until World War II the United States had not had a national intelligence agency that included spies engaged in gathering information within foreign countries. The attitude was that ''it was not gentlemanly to read other people's mail.'' As World War II approached, however, President Franklin D. Roosevelt realized that such an agency was needed, and he created the Office of the Coordinator of Information. This became the OSS when the war began. The OSS was the forerunner of the postwar Central Intelligence Agency (CIA).

British agents were under the overall command of Sir William Stevenson, code-named Intrepid.

Sir Claude Dansey was his top aide and in direct charge of agents out of London. A Canadian by birth, Stevenson was also a hero of World War I and between the wars had become intelligence aide to Winston Churchill. Unknown to United States citizens, during much of World War II Stevenson maintained his headquarters in New York City.

Stevenson and Donovan worked closely together—although unfortunately their underlings did not—not only to recruit and train agents to aid the French resistance, but also to establish a worldwide intelligence network. As part of this network the Allies had officials strategically placed in various neutral countries around the globe. One of these American officials was Allen Dulles, who was stationed in Berne, Switzerland, and actually directed OSS operations throughout Europe from there. Dulles, future head of the CIA, was frequently accused by the British of creating as many problems as he solved in attempting to aid the resistance networks in France.

For one thing Dulles fully agreed with President Roosevelt's opposition to General Charles de Gaulle. Neither Roosevelt nor Dulles thought that de Gaulle was the legitimate head of the French government in exile, nor did they think de Gaulle should head the post-liberation French government. Consequently, Dulles strongly opposed

Jean Moulin's efforts to unify all of the French-resistance networks under a National Resistance Council that would swear allegiance to de Gaulle.

One of Moulin's major jobs in establishing this council had been to wean several resistance leaders away from OSS control. This was especially difficult when Dulles, through his OSS agents, seemed to be able to furnish unlimited money and much-needed supplies, while the British and de Gaulle's Free French could not.

The British on their part finally reached the point of accusing the OSS of trying to take over the whole of the resistance movement, something that was especially galling to the British because the Americans were Johnny-come-latelies to the spy game and had learned virtually everything they knew from the British.

Stevenson and Donovan spent much of their time trying to resolve these difficulties. Their job, especially before the United States entered the war, was further complicated by J. Edgar Hoover, head of the United States Federal Bureau of Investigation (FBI).

The Suspicious Hoover

The FBI was not involved in gathering foreign intelligence. It had the responsibility of guarding the internal security of the United States. But who was to say what this meant? J. Edgar Hoover was a dedicated patriot. He was also a fiercely protective man as far as the FBI and its duties were concerned. He regarded *any* clandestine activity that took place within the borders of the United States—even if it was by a friendly nation such as Great Britain—as a threat to American security.

When Britain's Sir William Stevenson set up shop in New York City and began to work with Wild Bill Donovan, who was then called U.S. Coordinator of Information, Hoover regarded both men and their intelligence operation with great suspicion. Stevenson's intelligence headquarters was disarmingly called the British Security Coordinator (BSC), but it did not take Hoover and his FBI agents long to discover its true function. Donovan's role also did not fool Hoover for very long.

Hoover did not want any foreign power's intelligence agents either training or operating in the United States. He also resented the appointment of Donovan to a newly created American agency that might one day threaten the power and authority of the FBI. Consequently, Hoover immediately began setting up roadblocks to hamper Stevenson's and Donovan's activities. These roadblocks frequently took the form of a total lack of cooperation between the FBI's agents and British agents.

Hoover's attitude soon led to what can only be regarded as one of the biggest intelligence blunders of the war. It involved a British double agent named Dusko Popov, who tried, unsuccessfully, to warn the United States about Japanese plans to attack Pearl Harbor.

V

The Spy Who Predicted Pearl Harbor

DUSKO POPOV WAS not the kind of spy who blended into the scenery. In fact quite the opposite. He was a colorful man with extravagant appetites that he did not hesitate to satisfy. He loved wine, women, song, and all manner of lush living. Nevertheless, he was respected by his peers as a topflight espionage agent.

In intelligence circles Popov has long been regarded as the role model for James Bond, the hero in Ian Fleming's highly successful series of books and motion pictures about agents and double agents. Fleming never denied this. Nor did Popov.

Popov was actually a double agent whose primary loyalties were to Great Britain, France, and the United States. A Croatian (Croatia is part of Yugoslavia) by birth, Popov was a high-living law student at Freiburg University in southern Germany in the late 1930s. When World War II began, Popov was back in his native Belgrade living the life of a man about town. There he was recruited for service in German intelligence.

Popov, however, was an ardent Yugoslav nationalist and opposed to Hitler and his Nazi movement. Consequently, he reported his recruitment by the Abwehr to the British embassy in Belgrade. There a British intelligence officer suggested that Popov go ahead and join the German intelligence service but report all of his assignments to the British—in short, become a double agent. This Popov did.

Popov's first assignment for the Abwehr was to find out which French officials would most likely collaborate with the Germans when Germany invaded France. This information was easy enough to get. Popov had numerous friends in Yugoslav diplomatic circles, and the British also had detailed information on potential high-ranking French collaborationists. When Popov gave his report to the Abwehr, it confirmed in every detail the information the Abwehr had already received from its agents in Paris. Popov had passed his first test by the Germans with flying colors.

When France fell, the Abwehr seriously considered sending Popov there, but the French resistance had not yet become a serious menace, and it was decided he would be more valuable to Hitler's Third Reich in England. Although Great Britain had been driven from the Continent by the Nazis, the British under Churchill gave no sign of surrendering. German intelligence needed to know the state of British morale. Was the civilian population ready to get out of the war? Specifically, the Abwehr wanted Britain's Order of Battle and the island fortress's defense plans for its southern coast. When Popov told his British case officer the kind of information the Abwehr was seeking, it confirmed British suspicions that Germany was planning to invade Great Britain in the near future.

A major advantage for the Germans in sending Popov to England was that he would not have to go in secretly by parachute or be landed on a British beach. Since Yugoslavia was neutral, he could go in openly as a Yugoslav businessman. The advantage to the British in having Popov in London was obvious. He could keep British intelligence advised immediately of the Abwehr's requests for information and thus divulge Germany's military plans.

Popov in England

Popov got to London via Lisbon, Portugal. In London he was interrogated for several days by British intelligence officers who feared he might actually be a German agent. When they were satisfied that he was what he claimed to be, a bona fide double agent working for the British, Popov was allowed to go to work. They gave him the code name Tricycle.

Tricycle set up offices in a building near Piccadilly Circus. On the office door was the sign: TARLAIR LTD. EXPORT IMPORT. His staff was made up of other double agents, but all of these, unlike Popov, were male and female victims of the Double-Cross System—German agents who had been caught and "turned" by the British.

The first major job of Tricycle and his staff was to supply the Germans with enough misinformation (or disinformation, as it is called) about British military strength to encourage Germany to call off its Operation Sea Lion—the invasion of Britain. When Germany canceled Operation Sea Lion in the autumn of 1940, Popov received much private approval in British intelligence circles.

Public acclaim, of course, went to the valiant men of the Royal Air Force who had defeated the Luftwaffe in the aerial Battle of Britain. For Operation Sea Lion to be successful, the Luftwaffe would have to have control of the air.

The Abwehr continued to be more than satisfied with the work of Popov in London. For one thing he had been the only one of its agents who had been able to set up a regular spy cell there, but a cell whose members—unknown to the Germans— were all double agents supplying the Abwehr with disinformation carefully monitored by the British.

Popov in the United States

So satisfied were Popov's German case officers with his espionage work that early in 1941 they decided to send him to the United States. The cover of virtually all of the German agents in the United States had been broken by the FBI. Popov's job would be to recruit new agents and set up new cells. Again he could go as a Yugoslav businessman, although before he left Britain Popov managed to secure a position in Yugoslav offices in New York as a propaganda specialist. The Abwehr was impressed with this new job because it would also enable Popov to supply Germany with information about American war preparedness. Was the United States going to enter the war or not? If so, in what state was its military machine? What about American civilian morale? Were the isolationists as powerful as they appeared to be?

In addition to his general assignment Popov was also given a number of specific questions for which he was to supply the answers. He was startled to see that in order to answer several of the questions he would somehow have to get to Hawaii, or contact someone who had just come from there. Popov asked his case officer just who wanted the information about Hawaii. Japan, he was told. Japan, Italy, and Germany had formed the "Tokyo-Rome-Berlin Axis" (the Axis) as World War II allies, and Japan looked to Germany as a main source of military intelligence about the United States.

When Popov told the British about his reassignment to the United States, they reluctantly agreed he must go in order to keep from compromising his role as their double agent. British intelligence would not be out of touch with him, however. His British contact in New York would be Sir William Stephenson. The British also told him they would alert the FBI to his presence in New York. They emphasized that the questions regarding Hawaii should be turned over to Hoover and the FBI for the appropriate action.

On his way to the United States Popov was met by his Abwehr case officer in Lisbon. This time he was given a full page of questions about Hawaii that the Japanese wanted answered. They all had to do with the United States military installations at Pearl Harbor.

Popov commented that it looked as if the Japanese were going to attack Pearl Harbor. That seemed a distinct possibility, his case officer agreed.

But Popov objected that there was simply no way he could go off on a Hawaiian holiday as soon as he got to New York. That would arouse American suspicions. The case officer insisted that the Japanese needed the information immediately and that Popov should make every possible effort to obtain it.

Just before leaving Portugal for the United States Popov forwarded to London the additional questions he had received about Hawaii. This information should have been forwarded by the British as a Red Alert to the United States of a potential threat to Pearl Harbor, but British intelligence did not do so. The British assumed that when Popov turned over to J. Edgar Hoover a list of the questions he was supposed to answer by an on-the-ground inspection of Hawaii, Hoover would in turn alert President Roosevelt, or at least some of FDR's aides.

Later Britain's Sir John Masterman said, "Obviously it was for the Americans to make their appreciation and to draw their deductions from the [Tricycle] questionnaire rather than for us to do so. Nonetheless, we ought to have stressed its importance more than we did." This was especially true since the Tricycle questionnaire was, as Masterman also observed, "a somber warning of the subsequent attack on Pearl Harbor."

Popov turned over the questionnaire to the FBI in August of 1941 shortly after he arrived in the United States. He expected immediate action, but for days nothing happened. Popov began hounding the FBI, insisting that he at least be allowed to go to Hawaii. When he returned, American intelligence could dictate whatever false information they wanted him to send to Germany. This was exactly the way he had worked with the British, Popov pointed out, and they all vouched for the results.

Conflict with Hoover and the FBI

But Mr. Hoover wanted no part of either Mr. Popov or the British, who tried their best to put in a good word on Tricycle's behalf. Hoover did not trust the British, and he trusted Popov even less. Their beloved Tricycle, Hoover informed the British, was a German spy who had been palmed off on them, and they were trying to palm him off on Hoover. Actually Hoover distrusted any foreigner working in the United States as an intelligence agent. He also disliked Popov personally.

Disgusted, Popov decided to relieve some of his frustration by resuming the manner of living to which he was more accustomed. He took part of the $40,000 that had been given him by the Germans to set up a spy ring in Manhattan and bought a red convertible automobile. Then he and a beautiful blonde fashion model took off for Florida.

Such irresponsible and immoral action confirmed all of Hoover's suspicions about Popov. FBI agents were models of respectability and Hoover frowned on any country's agents who weren't. Hoover ordered one of these proper FBI agents to follow the immoral Tricycle and his girlfriend. He found them sunning themselves on the sands at a Miami beachfront hotel where they were registered as man and wife. The agent told Popov that he had better return to New York—alone—or the FBI would have him arrested on the grounds of transporting a woman across state lines for immoral purposes. Not wanting to destroy his role as Tricycle, the successful double agent, Popov angrily agreed. He put his girlfriend on an airplane and drove back to New York.

Upon his return Popov insisted on an audience with Hoover. He demanded to know what had been done about the questionnaire that clearly indicated the Japanese interest in Pearl Harbor as a target. Popov soon realized that absolutely nothing had been done about it.

Hoover countered by accusing Popov of being a German spy who was selling to the Abwehr the information he got from the FBI as well as from Stephenson's agents. Popov, Hoover charged, was using the money he got for selling such information to maintain his extravagant life style.

Angrily, Popov denied the accusation.

Then how could Popov afford the penthouse apartment he had rented on Park Avenue?

This, like the Florida trip, was with money the Germans had given him to set up a spy ring, Popov explained.

Then where were the spies? Hoover wanted to know. His FBI agents had reported that not a single spy had contacted Popov.

He was supposed to set up a *new* spy ring, Popov said. This meant new spies had to be recruited.

Was he recruiting them in Miami? the FBI chief asked.

Finally, Popov threw up his hands. He realized that Hoover had absolutely no intention of believing anything that Popov told him, either about himself or about the Pearl Harbor questionnaire. Popov strode out of Hoover's office.

After that interview Tricycle made no further effort to deal with the FBI. Stevenson's people gave him enough intelligence information to satisfy the Abwehr for the next several months, although it included not much more than facts from travel folders about Hawaii. Popov also spent much time at the New York public library where he digested stories about the United States economy and military preparedness from newspapers and periodicals, which he then included in his reports to Germany.

To further divert the Abwehr's attention, Popov also persuaded them to let him undertake espionage assignments in the Caribbean and South America. He was returning from one of these trips when he heard the news about the Japanese attack on Pearl Harbor on December 7, 1941. Dusko Popov, alias Tricycle, was not surprised although everybody else seemed to be. Then and afterward he firmly believed that J. Edgar Hoover was responsible for the fact that the Japanese surprised even the American top military command. As far as Popov was concerned the incriminating evidence that proved this point, the original Japanese questionnaire the Germans had given him that virtually named the time and place, was in British intelligence files. It was not until almost thirty years after the war that a provision of the British Official Secrets Act was relaxed, making it possible for a photocopy of this original questionnaire to be reprinted in Popov's autobiography about his experiences as the double agent Tricycle.

When the United States entered the war, Popov persuaded the Germans to let him return to England. He continued to be regarded by the Abwehr as their best agent there right up to the end of the war.

Back in England Tricycle did truly valuable work for the British by briefing agents who were about to be dropped into France to aid the resistance. By now he had much inside information about how the German secret police worked, and he was only too happy to pass this information along to the French underground. He also was active in debriefing Allied agents when they returned from France.

The Microdot

One of the most valuable espionage aids that was made available to the French resistance thanks to Popov was the microdot, or *mikropunkt* as the Germans called it. This was a photographic method of reducing a full-size page of writing to a piece of microfilm the size of a dot over an i or the period at the end of a sentence. A microdot could be read under a microscope or be enlarged to normal size with photographic enlarging equipment.

The microdot technique had been developed by the Germans. Popov was the first Abwehr agent to be let in on the secret and was given a sample of a microdot by his case officer when Popov was sent to the United States. Popov in turn showed it to the FBI, who at first regarded it as an interesting toy.

But when Popov returned to England and showed the microdot to British intelligence, they were immediately aware of its espionage possibilities. British scientists set to work developing their own system of photographically miniaturizing pages of handwritten or typed messages. When they had it perfected it was immediately made available to the French resistance.

Marie-Madeleine, alias Hedgehog, the head of the Noah's Ark resistance network, was one of the first underground agents to be furnished with microdot equipment. Before she was forced to flee to England she put it to excellent use. When she arrived in England she reported to the SOE that she had found the microdot far superior to secret inks, which sometimes remained permanently invisible or suddenly became visible shortly after they were used to write messages. Even the best of secret inks she had found not wholly reliable, while the microdot was not only reliable but versatile. It needn't simply replace dots in a normal letter. It could be stuck to an agent's skin or placed inside a hollow tooth or sewn into the lining of clothing. If an agent were caught, the microdot could be swallowed or easily destroyed.

VI

Missing, Presumed Dead

ON THE EVENING of May 11, 1944, a French resistance radio operator in Rambouillet, a town some thirty miles southwest of Paris, received an urgent message from intelligence headquarters in England. Earlier that day on a bombing mission to Chaumont, France, a United States B-24 Liberator bomber had been shot down near the village of Coulanges Les Sablons. Air crews from the U.S. 487th Bomb Group, who had returned to England from the mission, reported seeing several parachutes open from the Liberator on its way down. It was vital, the message said, to rescue any survivors—especially the pilot, if he had indeed escaped. The reason: the pilot was the commander of the 487th Bomb Group.

Several members of the Rambouillet resistance group went immediately into action to organize a rescue squad. The radio message had not said so, but as members of the French Forces of the Interior (FFI), the resistance fighters knew that D-Day for the Allied invasion of France was only weeks away. Now was no time to risk having an American bomb group commander fall into the hands of the Germans. No one knew better than the FFI how brutally successful the Nazis were in extracting information from their captives, especially high-ranking and well-informed officers.

The immediate problem faced by the Rambouillet rescue squad was the fact that the area in which the Liberator had been shot down was a German stronghold. If the downed fliers had not already been captured, finding and removing them from the area would be a next to impossible undertaking. But the impossible rarely fazed the FFI, or "Fee Fee" as they were popularly called.

At great personal risk and against all resistance rules, a telephone call was made to an FFI leader in the town of Nogent-le-Rotrou. This was the only large town near the site of the bomber crash, and the only one with a telephone exchange. The local FFI leader was not available, but the telephone operator—also at great personal risk—reported that two officers from the downed plane had eluded capture and had been hidden by a local farmer in a stone stable near Coulanges Les Sablons. All of the other crew members had either been killed or captured, and the Germans were now combing the neighborhood for the two hiding fliers.

In Rambouillet the resistance radio operator then called British intelligence and reported that two of the missing aircrew, identities and ranks unknown, had been located and a rescue mission would soon be under way. If it was successful, a British Lysander aircraft should be alerted to fly to a previously designated farm field near Nogent-le-Rotrou to pick up the survivors.

Early the next morning several members of the Rambouillet FFI boarded a train for the short journey to Nogent-le-Rotrou. They did not travel in a group but singly to avoid mass capture. Arriving at Nogent-le-Rotrou early that afternoon, they were also met singly and provided with bicycles. Then, one by one, they rode to the village of Coulanges Les Sablons, where they assembled at the home of a local resistance member. Here they were given the exact location of the stone stable in which the downed fliers were being hidden. They waited until that night for the rescue attempt.

At midnight the would-be rescuers crept out of the house and made their way down a country road toward the farm and its stone stable. They went on foot and as silently as possible. Any French man or woman caught outdoors after curfew was liable to be shot. The Germans rigidly enforced this regulation.

An hour later the FFI members reached their goal. There was no moon. This helped the rescue effort but would hinder a pick-up plane from England. Lysander landings were usually made only on moonlit nights. The men approached the stable from several sides. Then they entered through its several doors. The ground floor was empty, as they expected. A ladder was raised toward the opening leading to the hayloft. Only a single man could climb this ladder, and he did so with extreme caution, fearing the Americans might be armed and taking him for a German and open fire.

"Ami! Ami!" the man climbing the ladder whispered, reassuring the fliers that he was their friend.

But there was no response.

Cautiously still, the Frenchman climbed into the loft. It was only partially filled with hay, and otherwise apparently empty. He called to his friends below, who now came clattering up the ladder. Perhaps the fliers were hiding in the sparse hay. They searched through it without success. The Americans had fled—or worse, they had been captured.

The members of the FFI rescue party regretted having to question the farmer who owned the stable, since he had already risked his life hiding the fliers. Now he would be risking it again by talking with them. But there was no choice. They must find out what had happened.

The Tragic Mission

The target of the 487th Bomb Group on that sunny spring day of May 11, 1944, had been the railroad marshaling yards at Chaumont. They had originally been scheduled to fly in at about 22,000 feet and Colonel Beirne Lay, Jr., commander of the group, had not been assigned to go on the mission. When their flight altitude had been lowered to about half the original height, however, Colonel Lay realized that an experienced flier would be needed to lead the mission and volunteered for the job. The copilot in the lead plane was Lieutenant Walter Duer.

To reach Chaumont it was necessary to fly down a narrow corridor of enemy anti-aircraft guns between Chartres and Chateaudun. Bombers straying out of this flak corridor would be subjected to some of the worst ack-ack (anti-aircraft) fire on the Continent. In addition, there was a German fighter-plane base at Chateaudun manned by some of the best fighter pilots left in the Luftwaffe.

Half way to Chaumont, Colonel Lay's B-24 Liberator was hit and severely damaged by flak. Within moments Lay knew they were going down. He gave the order to abandon ship.

Colonel Lay and Lieutenant Duer were the last men to bail out. Beneath them they counted eight other parachutes. Lay and Duer landed in a plowed field only a few hundred yards from the blazing wreck of their B-24. None of the other crew members were in sight.

As Lay and Duer gathered in their chutes, a French farmer and his teenage son approached them across the plowed fields. Other people, several of them German soldiers, moved toward the blazing bomber. Lay knew it was vital for him and Duer to take cover immediately. In preflight briefings intelligence officers had told them that the first half hour was the most important for downed fliers trying to avoid being captured. And if they could remain hidden for twenty-four hours, their chances of eventual escape grew by ninety percent. Forty-eight hours without being picked up and they would probably be home free.

Lay and Duer headed for a nearby wheat field. There the Frenchman and his son found them lying partially hidden by the three-foot-high wheat. The Frenchman told them to lie there for ten minutes, then crawl to a nearby hedgerow and move along its base to the road across from a stone stable. If they could make their way immediately across the road, they could hide in the stable. He would see them there that night.

The two downed fliers made the journey to the stable successfully. Once hidden in the loft, however, they were almost detected by a German search party. But the German soldier sent up the ladder to search the loft only glanced about him quickly from the loft opening, apparently fearing he might be shot by the escaped fliers if they were there and armed. He then descended in equal haste.

As they lay waiting for night to fall and the farmer's return, Lay and Duer took a compass and a silk waterproof map from an escape kit that each flier carried in a pocket in the leg of his coveralls. They roughly located the area where they had been shot down and then worked out a route that would lead them south toward the

Pyrénées Mountains. They had also learned from intelligence officers as well as from other successful escapees that if they could make their way to the Pyrénées and cross them into neutral Spain, they would eventually be returned to England.

That night the Frenchman and his son returned. They were carrying a sack full of food and wine. They also told them that several of the other crew members had already been captured by the Germans. Risking his life, the farmer had alerted the mayor of the village that the two American fliers were being hidden in the farmer's stable. Although Lay and Duer did not know it at the time, the Coulanges Les Sablons mayor had passed the word to the local resistance organization at Nogent-le-Rotrou.

But now the farmer was eager for Lay and Duer to leave his stable. The entire area was crawling with *Allemands* (Germans), and the stable would doubtless again be searched, this time more thoroughly. If any sign of the fliers was found in the stable, the farmer and perhaps his whole family would be summarily shot. He would, however, risk hiding them for twenty-four more hours.

The next night the farmer returned with another sackful of food. His son carried a second sack, this one filled with clothing. After they had changed into French peasant garb, the fliers would have to take their flying gear with them and bury it along the way. The farmer also indicated on their escape map the route they should follow south, emphasizing that they should avoid the German stronghold at Nogent-le-Rotrou. He assured them that once out of the immediate area if they asked a *curé* (parish priest) for help, they would probably be put in touch with the resistance and moved along by its members to Spain and freedom.

Colonel Lay and Lieutenant Duer left the stable at midnight. The farmer guided them in the right direction and wished them a final *Bonne chance!* (Good luck).

An hour later the Rambouillet FFI rescue squad arrived at the empty stone stable.

Resistance to the Rescue

Walking by night and sleeping in barns, fields, woods, or hedgerows by day, the two escapees traveled south for a week. Here and there a friendly farmer or curé fed them and let them rest briefly, but no one offered to put them in touch with the resistance. All of their benefactors, in fact, were terrified of the occupying German forces, and these forces seemed to be everywhere.

At the end of the week Lay and Duer reached the town of Oucques. Here, having had no food for twenty-four hours, they decided to walk boldly into a local hotel dining room and order breakfast. They would pay for it with the francs that were in their escape kits which they had brought with them.

But as soon as they were seated the proprietor told them abruptly that the dining room did not serve breakfast and ordered them to leave.

Across the street from the hotel was a church. In desperation Lay and Duer entered it and appealed to a priest for help. This time they hit pay dirt. At first, fearing that the two men were German agents, the curé was reluctant to help them. But then, convinced by their American accents that they were legitimate, he set the resistance wheels in motion.

For the rest of that day Lay and Duer were hidden in the church. That evening they were led across the street to the very hotel from which they had been ejected that morning. The inn keeper, a M. Jacques, explained that when they had entered the dining room there was also a French policeman there eating breakfast, a known German collaborator. M. Jacques was afraid that the two Americans might betray themselves by speaking English, so he had hurriedly made them leave. But now they were in safekeeping. The FFI would take charge of them.

Soon afterward Lay and Duer were hustled out of the hotel and hidden in a grain silo near the edge of town. There they remained for several more days. Twice a day food was brought to them from the hotel by resistance members. Then one morning two Frenchmen driving a panel delivery truck stopped outside the silo. Lay and Duer were quickly put into the back of the truck and driven out of town. After traveling along rural roads for several miles they passed through the tiny village of Mazangé. A mile outside Mazangé the delivery van finally stopped at an isolated farmhouse. Here they were greeted by the farmer, a M. Paugoy; his wife, Mme. Paugoy; their son, Georges; a hired girl, Denise; and several members of the FFI.

The FFI members assured Lay and Duer that it would only be a matter of days before they were back in England. Either the FFI would guide them to the Pyrénées or, better still, request a Lysander flight from England. The two escapees were, of course, delighted that their ordeal seemed to be nearing its end. But it was actually to be a matter of months before the FFI's promise was fulfilled.

Although the farmhouse was isolated, great care had to be taken so that the fliers were not seen by any passing German patrols. Several days after Lay and Duer arrived at the farm M. Paugoy returned from a trip into the village of Mazangé with tragic news. M. Jacques, the hotel keeper at Oucques, had been taken into custody by the Germans, who had heard that he had helped two American fliers escape. Later it was learned that M. Jacques was tortured and killed, but he never divulged any information about Colonel Lay and Lieutenant Duer—even though the Germans gouged out his eyes.

While they waited to be returned to England, the two fliers were allowed to work in the fields as long as they remained some distance from the farmhouse. Stripped to the waist, they could pass as hired hands when seen at a distance. M. Paugoy cautioned them, however, against singing or talking loudly in English. If anyone seemed like they might approach them, the pilots were told to walk slowly away and disappear into the woods. Lay and Duer actually welcomed the physical activity, since it helped keep their minds off worrying about their families back in the United States and wondering what word they had received about the missing fliers. But as the days passed and the days grew into weeks, the two men became more and more impatient over the interminable delay.

The reason for the delay soon became clear.

The Allied landings in Normandy were imminent, and the FFI throughout France was too busy preparing to assist the invasion forces to help Lay and Duer conclude their escape.

M. Paugoy urged patience. Once the Americans and the English landed, he told them, the Fee Fee would deliver the fliers directly to their friends.

The waiting continued.

Home At Last

Then, early on the morning of June 6, 1944, M. Paugoy burst into the fliers' bedroom to announce that D-Day had arrived! The news had been picked up on a clandestine radio, and the FFI spread the word throughout the countryside. M. Paugoy himself had become so emboldened by the news that he had taken his own old radio out of hiding and had it turned on at top volume in the kitchen.

Colonel Lay and Lieutenant Duer leaped out of bed and dashed into the kitchen. They were about to be liberated!

But they were too optimistic. More days and weeks passed while the Allies consolidated their landings and began to battle their way into France through the difficult *bocage*, or hedgerow country. Lay and Duer were all for starting off on their own to contact the advancing Americans, but M. Paugoy as well as the head of the local FFI cautioned them against such an effort. First of all they would have to make their way through the German lines and would probably be captured. And if they eluded the Germans they would still be out of uniform. Dressed as peasants, the two fliers would not be recognized by their countrymen and might be shot by them in error or by the Germans as spies.

The two fliers continued to wait, and as they waited they were impressed with the vast number of FFI resistance fighters that had sprung up throughout the local area. M. Paugoy's farm, they discovered, was not just a hiding place for refugees. It was also a regular arsenal. Arms and ammunition had been secretly dropped by British bombers during the past months and hidden away by the Paugoy family. These arms drops now increased, and the FFI streamed onto the farm to obtain weapons and ammunition. Lay and Duer volunteered to act as supply sergeants in passing out this matériel.

Finally, on a hot day in mid-August, the sound of artillery fire could clearly be heard at the farmhouse. Shortly afterward more than a dozen armed to the teeth resistance fighters roared up in two ancient automobiles. The Americans under

General George Patton were within about thirty kilometers (20 miles) of the farm, they announced. It was time for Colonel Lay and Lieutenant Duer to join their comrades.

Lay and Duer said fond farewells to the Paugoy family and promised faithfully to return after the war. Then they were driven off in a cloud of dust toward the American lines. Resistance fighters stood on the battered sedans' running boards and even sat on their hoods, their guns cocked and ready to blaze away at any stray Germans. None were encountered.

The first Americans they saw were members of an armored infantry platoon. For a moment it was touch and go whether the Americans would open fire, but then the GI's saw the FFI armbands the resistance fighters were wearing and the crisis passed. Already the Yanks had come to realize what valuable allies the FFI were.

When the resistance escort realized that Lay and Duer were in safe hands, they saluted, piled back into their battered cars and roared away. The GI's turned the two fliers over to their commanding officer. A few moments later they were in a jeep on their way back to battalion headquarters. There they were questioned briefly by a major to make certain they were who they said they were. A radio message to Air Force headquarters confirmed their identity. They spent that night at division headquarters, and the next day were taken to the Ninth Air Force headquarters in France. There they were interrogated at greater length, after which they were flown to England. Within a few weeks they were on their way back to the United States for thirty days of R and R—rest and recuperation.

Colonel Lay and Lieutenant Duer were only two of literally thousands of Allied airmen and other refugees that the FFI and other French resistance fighters kept from falling into the hands of the Germans during the course of World War II.

VII

Escapees and Evaders

MOST OF THE FRENCH resistance networks helped shelter and smuggle out of France Allied soldiers and fliers who had escaped from German prisoner-of-war camps or who were evading capture after being shot down on bombing raids. There were several networks, however, that specialized in escape and evasion activities.

The Pat Line

The so-called Pat line was started by a Belgian named Albert-Marie Guérisse. Guérisse escaped to England when Belgium was overrun by the

Germans early in the war. In London he was taken in charge by the SOE, who turned him over to MI-9, which was just starting its operations as a command post for escapers and evaders. (The Americans later simply called such personnel escapees.)

At that time MI-9 had its headquarters in a room at London's Metropole Hotel. When the Metropole was severely damaged by a bomb in an air raid, Major N.R. Crockatt, who was in charge of MI-9, decided to move his operation to Beaconsfield, about twenty-five miles outside London. An interrogation center was maintained in the Marylebone area of London.

Major Crockatt, a wounded and much decorated hero of World War I, was assisted by a relatively small staff, the most noteworthy member of which was Captain C. Clayton Hutton. Hutton was a person of great imagination and ingenuity who designed virtually all of the first escape devices needed by POW's and downed fliers in their efforts to evade capture. These escape aids included maps printed on silk (so they wouldn't rustle when opened), a wide variety of compasses that could be easily concealed, miniature saws, water-purifying pills, miniaturized food and medicine packets, and several other devices. He then devised a compact, unbreakable box in which these aids could be packed. After much experimentation Hutton perfected an escape kit that could fit in the leg pocket of a flier's coveralls. Colonel Lay and Lieutenant Duer were each carrying such escape kits when they were shot down.

When the United States entered the war and the Eighth and Ninth Air Forces arrived in Great Britain, their intelligence officers recognized an immediate need for Hutton's escape kits as well as information about escape and evasion techniques on the Continent. Major W. Stull Holt, a former historian at Johns Hopkins University, was the liaison officer between the United States Air Force and MI-9. Thanks largely to Holt and the officials at Beaconsfield, there was close and friendly cooperation between the two services all through the war.

MI-9 was keenly interested in the Belgian, Albert-Marie Guérisse, because he was determined to return to the Continent and engage in some kind of resistance activity. MI-9 officers outlined their plans for setting up escape and evasion networks, and Guérisse leaped at the chance to establish one.

After several weeks of training, Guérisse was put ashore by boat at the French town of Etang de Canet. Almost immediately, however, he was picked up by a Vichy policeman. To avoid being shot as a spy, Guérisse told the policeman that his name was Patrick Albert O'Leary, a downed Canadian flier who was trying to evade capture.

"Patrick A. O'Leary" was arrested and put in jail at Nîmes. But in a few days he escaped and headed for northern France. There he made contact with other resistants and together they began to form their escape line. Setting up safe houses as they moved south, O'Leary and his friends soon had established a line that led from northern France through Paris, down to Vichy, and from there across the Pyrénées into Spain.

MI-9 called this the PAO line, using the initials from Guérisse's cover name, but unofficially it was always called the Pat line because that was what Guérisse-O'Leary's comrades called him. During the first year that it was in operation some six hundred soldiers, fliers, and volunteers for de Gaulle's fledgling Free French forces were successfully moved along the Pat line. From then on the number of its "passengers" continued to grow until 1943 when this flow was temporarily disrupted due to German infiltration of the resistance networks.

The Comet Line

The Comet line was established by another Belgian, a school teacher's daughter named Andrée "Dédée" de Jongh. Just twenty-five, Dédée de

Jongh was a commercial artist but had been trained as a nurse. One of her girlhood idols was also a nurse, Edith Cavell, a British World War I heroine.

Edith Cavell had been in charge of a hospital in Brussels, Belgium, in 1915, when the Germans occupied the city. She not only aided the wounded but also assisted some two hundred Allied soldiers to escape into the Netherlands. Arrested and tried by the Germans as a spy, Edith Cavell's last words before she was shot by a firing squad were: "Patriotism is not enough."

With her country once again occupied by the Germans, Dédée de Jongh did not think that mere patriotism was enough either, so she and a group of her young friends organized an escape route that ran from Brussels, down across France, and into the Pyrénées. There she enlisted the aid of Basque mountain guides to help her charges escape to freedom.

Ironically, when Dédée first offered her services to the British they suspected her of being a German agent. But MI-9 had her thoroughly investigated—"vetted" in the British phrase—and found her to be a genuine resistant.

Because Dédée and her colleagues referred to their charges as Packages, their line was first called Postman. But due to the speed with which they transported escapees out of France and into

Spain the line soon was renamed Comet.

The Comet line had the unique distinction of being operated almost exclusively by young men and women in their teens and twenties. They averaged handling about fifty escapees a month all during the war. The Comet line specialized in aiding escaping aircrews, and in one instance succeeded in moving the entire seven-man crew of a Royal Air Force bomber from northern France to Spain in a week.

Record Return

As it turned out, what was probably the fastest such return recorded was that of a young RAF fighter pilot shot down over France in the summer of 1943. As related by British historians M.R. Foot and J.M. Langley, on a Saturday evening this young pilot became engaged to a girl at a dance at London's Savoy Hotel. He then told his fiancée he would again meet her at the Savoy the following Saturday. On Monday he was shot down over northern France. Parachuting to safety, the pilot was unable to avoid landing on the roof of a large greenhouse on the spacious grounds of a chateau. He was unhurt, and the gardener—a resistance member—hid him in a shed and began cleaning away the parachute and broken glass.

While the gardener was thus occupied, the

French count whose chateau it was appeared and demanded that he be taken to the pilot. The count then brought the young flier into the chateau, where he was entertained for several days. Toward the end of the week the pilot was awakened in the middle of the night and hurried to the chateau's park, where a Lysander soon landed to fly him back to England.

The returned RAF fighter pilot kept his date at the Savoy and later he and his fiancée were married. The count, the young flier learned after his rescue, was also a resistance member and ran his chateau as a safe house for MI-9. It was, in fact, one of the organization's most successful safe houses.

The pilot was ordered to spend the next several months off flight duty to avoid the chance of his again being shot down, captured, and perhaps divulging the count's activities. This was common practice in MI-9's handling of returned evaders. The American Air Force avoided all such risks by returning its escapees to the United States. It was able to do so because of its abundance of trained fliers. The manpower-short RAF could afford no such luxury. Escaping American fliers were also promoted and decorated with the Air Medal or Distinguished Flying Cross before being returned to what was called the Zone of the Interior for thirty days of R and R. The prospect of such handsome treatment if they returned may well have acted as an added incentive for downed American fliers to try to escape from the Continent.

The Shelburne Line

There was one unique escape line that did not go into Spain. This was the line code-named Shelburne, a name whose derivation is now lost. The Shelburne line had what were called collection points at Paris and Rennes. From these points escapees were moved to various ports on the English Channel, where they were picked up and taken by motor gunboats—similar to American torpedo or PT boats—to Falmouth or Weymouth in southern England.

The Shelburne line was started late in the war, but it handled several hundred escapees successfully. It was especially noteworthy for the bravery of the British gunboat crews who came ashore and collected their charges from the French ports right under the German guns.

The Marie-Claire Line

The Marie-Claire line was not so much a line as it was a one-woman operation. Most of the resistance networks that specialized in escape and evasion work used women to accompany their charges down across France because a woman accompanied by one or several men was much less conspicuous than several men traveling together. Marie-Claire, however, made no effort to be inconspicuous. In fact quite the opposite.

Marie-Claire was actually Mary Lindell, a British woman born in Surrey in 1895. She too had been a nurse in World War I and decorated for bravery. After that war she married a Frenchman and became the Comtesse de Milleville. She had been living in France for many years when World War II began, and in 1940 was a well-known society matron with three teenage children.

When the Germans occupied Paris, the countess continued to do Red Cross work in several hospitals, boldly wearing her British medal ribbons so there was never any doubt about where her loyalties lay. Nevertheless, when she appeared one day with a special request at the office of the German Commander of Paris, General Heinrich von Stülpnagel, she was received politely.

The tale the countess told von Stülpnagel was that there were a number of children in Paris who had been separated from their parents when the war began and the parents fled to unoccupied France. To reunite these families, the countess said, she needed travel permits and gasoline ration

coupons so she and her teenage children could
escort the temporarily orphaned children in her
two limousines into unoccupied France. Von
Stülpnagel graciously arranged to grant the countess's request.

Promptly she began an escort service, but not
for these mythical orphans. Instead she carried
British escapees to Marseilles, where she turned
them over to the Noah's Ark network, who then
spirited them out of the country. Recognizing the
countess's highly independent nature and not
wanting to tamper with the success of her unique
operation, Marie-Madeleine made no effort to enlist her as a regular member of the Ark.

Eventually the countess was picked up by the
Gestapo but not before she had helped a number
of refugees to escape. She was still treated with
great consideration even after her arrest and only
sentenced to a brief term in the French prison at
Fresnes. When she was released, she herself
made her way into Spain disguised as an elderly
governess in charge of several teenagers—her
own children—and from there was transported to
England. There she went to work for MI-9.

The Toulouse Line

Another unique French escape line, this one
nameless, was formed by a Jewish resistance

group in Toulouse. During the first half of World War II, many Central European Jews fleeing Hitler and his Nazis went first to France and then to Spain. From there they hoped to emigrate to the United States. Some thirty thousand Jews saved themselves in this fashion.

But when Germany occupied the whole of France, Hitler also ordered the mass deportation of all Jews in France to German concentration camps. Thousands of Jews were then forced to go underground and seek a resistance escape line into Spain. To meet their needs the Toulouse resistance group was formed. During the rest of the war, despite intense surveillance by Vichy French police and German border patrols, the Toulouse network smuggled some 7,500 Jews from France into Spain. Among them were at least six hundred children and teenagers.

While Spanish officials were willing to accept these Jewish refugees, they wanted them to pass quickly through their country and not become permanent residents. Spain's Foreign Minister, Jordana y Sousa, in fact stated, "They should pass through our country like light through glass, leaving no trace."

In Spain some of the Jews were briefly herded into concentration camps—one notorious one was called Miranda de Ebro—but most were sent on to Portugal and the United States. By 1945 some 40,000 Jews escaped from France and through Spain but no more than a few thousand were in Spain at one time.

Escape Through Spain!

This inflow of Jews into Spain competed with the inflow of Allied airmen—especially U.S. fliers—as well as young Frenchmen who were fleeing forced labor in Germany. In fact, during 1943–1944 when American day-bombing raids over the Continent grew to massive proportions, those fliers who were shot down, picked up by the French, and smuggled into Spain increased to what the Spanish regarded as an alarming degree. During such air raids the French began to hold what they called parachute parties. When a raid began, the French looked for parachutes coming from a disabled plane. Then, sometimes in crowds and always on bicycles, the French would rush to the site of the landing Americans and spirit them out of sight before they could be captured by the Germans. The Americans were then quickly given a change of clothes and turned over to an escape line. British air raids were at night so there were far fewer parachute parties held for them.

To prevent Spain from closing its borders to

Allied airmen and escaping POW's—especially American airmen and POW's—the American Ambassador to Madrid, Carlton J.H. Hayes, opposed private welfare efforts on behalf of Jewish refugees in Spain. Hayes even went so far as to block support to welfare agencies that would assist by supplying funds for the smuggling of Jews across the Pyrénées. If these funds were cut off, the chances of escape by the Jews were also cut down.

But in the end Spain's borders were never closed to any escapers, evaders, Jews, or other refugees. Why Spain's dictator, Francisco Franco, permitted his country to be, what amounted to, an Allied sanctuary was never quite clear. Certainly his political sympathies were all with Hitler and Mussolini.

Franco had become the Fascist dictator of Spain in 1939, following a bloody civil war in which close to a million Spaniards were killed. This conflict has often been called the opening battle of World War II and a testing ground for Hitler's military machine. In the Spanish Civil War, Germany sided with Franco and his Fascists, while France and Russia sided with the freedom-fighting Loyalists. Great Britain and the United States remained neutral, but many British and American volunteers fought in the International Brigade against Franco.

When World War II began, Franco sided with Hitler and later sent Spain's elite Blue Division of some 47,000 "volunteers" to fight with the Germans against Russia. But Franco disagreed with Hitler over his Jewish policy and steadfastly remained neutral during the war.

Some said Franco believed himself to be of Jewish descent, as rumors persistently said he was. This would explain his own Jewish policy. As for his acceptance of Allied refugees, perhaps he was merely hedging his bets and hoping to be on the winning side when the war ended. There may also have been a monetary consideration involved. There were also persistant rumors in intelligence circles that Franco was paid for each Allied flier—as much as $10,000 a head it was said—who was repatriated to England via Spain, but these rumors have never been confirmed.

What is known is that Franco was always highly skillful in dealing with Hitler. Hitler did his utmost to get Spain to enter the war against England and thus close the entrance to the Mediterranean. But Franco flatly refused to do so, because of Spain's dire economy, Hitler's refusal to agree to Franco's territorial demands, and Franco's perception that the war was turning in favor of the Allies. This refusal was a major contribution to Germany's ultimate defeat. It was also a refusal that took courage, because at one point Hitler threatened to invade Spain by attacking Gibraltar. And when Germany occupied all of France, German troops took up positions along the Spanish frontier. Still Franco did not budge. He was, as historian Haim Avni has pointed out, the only European statesman of his era who dealt with Hitler without coming out second best. Early in the war Hitler and Franco met at the Spanish-French frontier. Hitler, who was used to dominating all conversations, was talked into the ground by Franco. Later Hitler wryly observed that he would "rather have several teeth pulled than have any more conversations with Franco."

How many Allied military escapees and evaders were actually smuggled out of France and into Spain will never really be known. Records during the war were poorly kept and reconstruction of them has been unsatisfactory. Combined official American and British sources indicate there were roughly 3,000 evading American fliers and several hundred escaping POW's who were processed through Spain. These same sources indicate there were roughly 2,500 evading British fliers and about 1,000 escaping POW's. (American and British escapees and evaders in all of the theaters of war totaled some 35,000, which amounts to several military divisions.)

Operating these escape and evasion lines was

not, of course, done without cost in human lives. Here, too, records are incomplete and unsatisfactory, since many of the resistants simply disappeared without a trace. Estimates of losses vary from the official five hundred to as many as several thousand. Historians Foot and Langley estimate that for every escapee who was safely returned to England a line operator lost his or her life.

The Black Year

In 1943 when disaster struck the other French resistance networks, German agents also succeeded in infiltrating the two major escape lines —Pat and Comet. Both Pat O'Leary and Dédée de Jongh were arrested by the Gestapo, tortured, and sentenced to die. These sentences were never carried out, but Dédée was sent to the Ravensbruck concentration camp and O'Leary to the concentration camp at Dachau. Miraculously, both survived the war.

Miraculously also, the escape lines and other resistance networks were not destroyed in 1943 but were rebuilt and became bigger and more effective than ever. By the approach of D-Day in Normandy there were as many as nine major resistance networks of all kinds battling the Germans from within France while the Allies attacked from without. In addition, numerous small but effective resistance groups had sprung up. One of the most successful of these was made up of fewer than seven hundred highly patriotic French men and women from an area near the Italian border. Its leader was an elementary school teacher, a man named Ange-Marie Miniconi. With headquarters in Cannes, Miniconi's heroic organization would play a key role in liberating the entire French Riviera.

VIII

Defiance on the Riviera

IN FRENCH THE TERM for railroad is *chemin de fer*, literally "road of iron." One who works on the railroad is thus called a *cheminot*. Early in the war French railway workers or *cheminots* formed their own separate resistance network. Called the Fer Réseau, or iron network, it was one of the most effective in France. A man who worked closely with the Fer Réseau and eventually formed his own network was Ange-Marie Miniconi.

Like many French men and women at the start of the war, Miniconi was a member of the "whispering resistance." He muttered about the German occupation of his country but did not actually do much about it. Then the whispering began to grow in volume, and before long words of defiance became deeds of action against the Germans. This was a pattern followed by every resistant and resistance network in France. It was perhaps most clearly evident among the railway workers.

When the Nazis took over France they knew that it was essential that the railways be kept working. They were vital not merely for transporting troops and military matériel but also for transporting civilian goods so the nation's economy would keep running. The Germans therefore did their utmost to win over the French railway workers as collaborationists.

Railroad Sabotage

But the *cheminots* were a proud and independent breed of French worker. They were also smart. They knew that because of the nature of their work they—unlike most other French workers—could travel freely throughout the country. They also were quick to realize how important their services were to the Germans. But it took the *cheminots* some months before they quietly began to take advantage of their key situation. Gradually, France's well-regulated and highly dependable rail system began to break down. Goods or freight shipments scheduled for one part of France wound up somewhere else. This was done simply by switching official bills of lading from one freight car to another. Constant delays began to develop as a result of right-of-way signals being stuck on red when they should have been changed to green.

Success bred success with the *cheminots*, as it did with other resistants. Soon vital switches were not thrown when they were scheduled to be thrown and serious derailments occurred. Journey boxes were not greased on freight-car axles, and soon wheels froze to a grinding halt. Rails were greased on downhill runs, causing collisions or pileups. Loads on flatcars would be improperly secured so they would slide off when a train rounded a curve or came to a sudden stop.

The Germans usually found it impossible to pin the blame for these "mistakes" on any individuals, so they put guards everywhere possible and threatened reprisals against railway controllers regardless of whether they were responsible for the accidents. But there weren't enough men in the German army to guard every mile of track even though they tried to do this with armored trains. The confusion continued to grow.

Saboteurs compounded the confusion when they began to blow up great stretches of track as well as key bridges. This latter work was, of course, highly dangerous, since men and women caught—or even suspected—of engaging in it were instantly shot. Hundreds of resistants died in this way. It was as a railway saboteur that Ange-Marie Miniconi underwent his baptism of fire as a resistance fighter.

Mail Sabotage

Young Miniconi was the son of a French mailman. The elder Miniconi, like many postal workers, also played a key role in the resistance movement. He and his wife allowed their home near Nice to be used as a letterbox or drop and engaged in other widespread resistance activities. The French Postal, Telegraph, and Telephone Service, like the railway system, was spread throughout the country and thus formed a ready-made network. Its members smuggled resistance correspondence and supplies. They also furnished the resistance with copies of enemy telegrams and any other German and Italian correspondence that might prove helpful.

The Miniconis Become Resistants

While Ange-Marie Miniconi was certainly aware of his parents' activities, he himself did not become an active resistant until midway in the war. Later his own wife and his five brothers—the youngest only a teenager—were all active in the resistance, so for the Miniconis fighting the Germans became a family affair.

Ange-Marie and his wife, Claire, were in their late twenties when the war began. They had two young sons, Felix-Henri and Guy. Both Ange-Marie and Claire were teachers and had been hired as a team to teach in the remote village of Peille in 1934. They had been there ever since.

The village of Peille and Ange-Marie Miniconi were all well suited to each other. Located in a mountainous area near the French-Italian border, Peille was a self-sufficient town whose citizens had a reputation for independence. They had bluntly refused to accept interference by outside authority. Peille's village motto dated back to the Middle Ages. It was *Vivere Liberi aut Mori*, live in freedom or die. This pretty well summed up Miniconi's philosophy—in addition to which he and his wife were confirmed pacifists.

The Miniconis were excellent teachers. Like her husband, Claire taught in the Peille elementary school, where she also served as headmistress, and together they succeeded in turning out students who graduated with honors where students had seldom even graduated before. The townspeople were more than satisfied with the strict but just Miniconi and his somewhat more congenial wife. But already problems lay ahead for the prickly pacifist Ange-Marie.

Shortly after he had been graduated with honors from the Nice teachers' college in the 1920s, Ange-Marie had been called up for the eighteen months compulsory military service then in effect in France. Since he had been such a brilliant student, it was expected that he would apply for officers' candidate training. But Ange-Marie bluntly refused, stating his pacifist views and deliberately failing the OCS qualifying test. His military superiors branded Ange-Marie as "Uncooperative," and his reputation as a troublemaker followed him until he was discharged from the service a year and a half later.

Miniconi happily returned to civilian life and teaching and continued in that role up to 1940 when the bad news of the German invasion of France arrived in Peille. Since Peille was in the unoccupied zone, however, Miniconi, his wife, and their townspeople friends were at first little bothered by the Nazi takeover. But as remote as Peille was, the fiercely independent little mountain village could not remain isolated forever. Nor could the fiercely independent Ange-Marie Miniconi.

Miniconi felt the long arm of the Vichy government in the winter of 1941. Soon after the Germans invaded the Soviet Union, Vichy Premier Pétain authorized a Volunteer French Legion to fight alongside the Nazis in Russia. Since Peille had the worst record of any town in its region for cooperating with the Vichy government, a recruiting officer was sent into the village to try and enlist "volunteers" to join the new French Legion. The recruiter soon learned that Miniconi was regarded as a leader in the village and tried to get him to enlist. Miniconi, of course, refused.

Early in 1942 Miniconi was again pressured to volunteer. This time the offer was indeed tempting. As a schoolteacher Miniconi earned 1,250 francs ($25) a month, and his wife even less. He was offered a captaincy in the Legion and a salary of 13,000 francs ($260) a month. Unhesitatingly, Miniconi again refused.

One of the reasons Miniconi was so stubborn was because of the changes he had already seen in the school textbooks that were furnished by the state. His wife had been ordered to remove all of the old textbooks from the school and distribute new ones. In the new books French and German history had been rewritten, showing Hitler and Pétain and the French collaborationists in a favorable light and condemning all anti-Vichy sentiments. The Spanish Civil War was also depicted as a victory for democratic government—a distortion that especially offended Miniconi, since some of his college classmates had died fighting as volunteers on the side of the Loyalists.

The Miniconis managed to salvage some of the old textbooks and continued to teach their students from them. They also refused to place pictures of Pétain in all of the school classrooms. When firmly ordered to do so by visiting school authorities, Miniconi found several postage stamps bearing Pétain's portrait and stuck these on the walls.

The Jean-Marie Group

In the summer of 1942 Miniconi was summoned by the regional education authorities to appear at a hearing in Nice. There he and his wife were accused of obstructing the work of Marshal Pétain. With no chance to defend themselves, the Miniconis were fired from their jobs in Peille and ordered to take teaching jobs in separate schools in Cannes. They were both also placed under official surveillance.

In Cannes Miniconi began to make tentative inquiries about resistance activities. He immediately encountered half a dozen resistants who had already carried out a number of individual acts of railway sabotage. These men and women were looking for a leader to coordinate their activities. Miniconi seemed to be that man. It was out of this small nucleus that the resistance network that became known as Groupe Jean-Marie was born. The name was simply a code name variation of Miniconi's first name, Ange-Marie.

Since several of the first members of the Jean-Marie Group were *cheminots*, other new members were also recruited from among freight yard and railroad repair shop workers. The group's first action was also against the railroads. On November 2, 1943, they derailed an ammunition train at LaBocca. A short time later they destroyed a lengthy section of railroad track at Anthéor. Then in quick succession they struck railway installations at Mandelieu, La Source, and the outskirts of Cannes itself. Meanwhile, they extended their activities by destroying several gasoline dumps in the Cannes area and by capturing a valuable supply of arms and ammunition in a rural enemy supply depot near LaBocca.

By early 1944 Miniconi's Jean-Marie Group had expanded to several hundred resistants, and their leader began to encounter two of the major problems encountered by all growing resistance networks—security maintenance and the need for paramilitary supplies. The latter problem was solved when contact was made with the Free French in London, who prevailed upon British intelligence to make supply drops by parachute. The former problem Miniconi attempted to solve in an ingenious fashion.

Triangle Cells

Like the other resistance networks, the Jean-Marie Group was divided into cells, but these were small three-person, or "triangle," cells. The three people in a triangle knew each other, of course, but its leader knew only the leader of one other cell and only by a code name or number. Thus if a member who was not the leader of a triangle cell was picked up by the Germans he or she could only betray the two other members in his or her own triangle cell. The leader of each cell could also betray his or her two other cell members as well as the leader of one other cell. But in order to find out who this second leader was the Germans would have to be able to decipher that person's code name or number.

Cells were grouped into larger units called sections. Each section was composed of four triangles and a leader. Four sections and a leader formed a detachment, and four detachments and a leader formed a company that had a commander and his aide or adjutant. A full company comprised 214 men and women. While Miniconi had been a reluctant soldier, he had obviously learned a few military lessons. His Jean-Marie Group was definitely set up along military lines. As the head of several companies, Miniconi was what amounted to a battalion commander, a title he steadfastly declined.

There has never been a one hundred percent foolproof way of preventing at least the partial destruction of a resistance network. As the other networks discovered, an enemy agent infiltrating a network could in time learn how many, if not most, of its members were. And even if a resistant did not know his resistance colleagues by their names or code numbers, meeting places were generally known and the Gestapo could be led to them. Nevertheless, Miniconi's system of hiding members' identities was so successful that only a handful of his Jean-Marie network members were ever picked up. After the war even Miniconi himself had an extremely difficult time identifying all of his wartime colleagues.

As the war progressed the Jean-Marie Group had to cope with two other major problems, problems that faced all non-collaborationist French civilians but were of even greater importance to active resistance fighters. These were transportation and food.

The Tricks of Travel

While many of the *cheminots* in the Jean-Marie Group had rail passes, they could not risk using them when they traveled from town to town for resistance meetings or to perform acts of sabotage. If they were picked up for questioning while traveling by train and they had no adequate explanation for their journey, their rail passes might be confiscated and their owners thrown in jail.

Consequently, most of the Jean-Marie Group —like most other resistants—traveled by bicycle. A fortunate few had old automobiles that had not been confiscated by the Germans. There was, of course, no gasoline available for normal civilian use, so most automobiles had been converted into *gasogènes*. These were vehicles whose engines had been modified to run on methyl gas made from burning wood, charcoal, or coal in the form of coke.

Gasogènes provided an effective but primitive and not wholly satisfactory means of travel. For one thing their engines had to be warmed up for twenty or thirty minutes before they would operate properly. They were also difficult to start in cold weather. In addition, room in the vehicle had to be provided for carrying the essential wood or charcoal or coke, which left little room for passengers.

Nevertheless, *gasogènes* were used fairly widely, and after the Allied invasion American and British troops were at first startled at the sight of them moving along rural roads or on city streets. A large inflatable bag was necessary to contain the gas created by the burning fuel, so at a distance a *gasogène* looked somewhat like a small observation balloon gliding along at hedgerow height.

The Black Market

The food problem, especially for resistants, was not so readily solved. Allied air drops had to be limited to war matériel—except in cases of extreme emergency—so the resistance networks had to live off their own meager rations, what they could obtain while moving through rural areas, and what they could buy or barter on the black market.

In the beginning the Jean-Marie Group was more successful than most other resistance networks in obtaining black-market supplies. The French Riviera, or Côte d'Azur—and especially Cannes—had a flourishing illegal food trade because in peacetime it was a major resort area, and when the war started many rich French men and women moved there to escape the Germans. They could afford to pay exorbitant prices for food, a fact that was not lost on the area's criminal element.

Black marketeers in France were called BOF's, which stood for *beurre, oeufs,* and *fromage* (butter, eggs, and cheese). Although Miniconi and his group disagreed with black marketeering in principle, they rationalized that the end they were seeking—defeating the Germans—justified the means of gaining that end, even if it meant dealing with the BOF's.

But when the Germans took over unoccupied France, they also took over Cannes, Nice, and every other point along the Riviera because these places were windows on the Mediterranean. The BOF's then shifted their trade to the German officers' messes, and the Jean-Marie Group had to return to the regular legal ration. This was scarcely enough to maintain a sedentary person and amounted to no more than an iron ration, a starvation diet for active resistants.

Starvation Rations

The regular civilian ration consisted of two ounces (50g) of bread per day. All pastries were illegal. Somewhat less than a pound (400g) of fats—butter, margarine, lard, or cooking oil—was allowed each person per month. About half a pound (200g) of cheese was also permitted per month. The meat ration was so small that the *cheminots* said it could be wrapped in a paper train or Métro transfer—if it didn't fall through one of the holes punched in the transfer.

The constant shortage of meat, fish, and fowl eventually resulted in the virtual disappearance of dogs and cats, which were obviously eaten although no one would admit to having done so. Newspapers ran articles cautioning people against eating cats, which were called "roof rabbits," because of the danger of contracting diseases. Real rabbits or hares were widely raised, frequently in people's kitchens because if they were allowed outside they would immediately be stolen.

Milk, except in rural areas, was always in short supply. Coffee was virtually nonexistant, so most people drank an ersatz brew made from grain, acorns, or any other available and potable substitute. Root vegetables such as potatoes, turnips, rutabagas, and carrots were readily available and comprised seventy-five percent of wartime diets. Malnutrition and illness from diet deficiencies were widespread.

Despite these problems—and they were severe, since food shortages sapped resistants' strength and morale—the Jean-Marie Group continued its widespread acts of sabotage right up to the time of the Allied invasion of Normandy in June of 1944. After they first received news of this invasion, Ange-Marie Miniconi had all he could do to prevent the members of his network from coming into the open and attacking German troops in southern France. Miniconi knew that if this happened his relatively small force would be slaughtered by the huge German military command that still occupied the whole of the Riviera. What they must wait for, Miniconi told his company commanders, was an invasion of southern France by the Allies. Miniconi had kept in close touch with the Free French in London and had been assured that such an invasion was scheduled by the Allies for sometime during the summer of 1944. When this occurred, Miniconi said, the Jean-Marie Group would be free to go into direct action against the Germans.

Allied Invasion

Meanwhile, the Jean-Marie Group's members concentrated on doing valuable espionage work to supply the Allies with information about German military installations and troop movements along the Riviera.

What they had to report to the Allies was good news. As the Normandy landings were consolidated and the Americans and British began to move inland, several divisions of German troops were removed from southern France and rushed north to bolster the Germans' crumbling English Channel defenses. There were still some 250,000 German troops manning the Riviera defenses, but they were the poorest troops in the Wehrmacht —war-weary veterans from the Russian front and soldiers recovering from battle wounds. Miniconi also reported that the number of German fighter aircraft in the area was down to fewer than two hundred planes, no match for the Allied air armada that was estimated to be some five thousand aircraft.

Nevertheless, Miniconi could not report that an Allied invasion of southern France would be a walkover, because the Germans had installed formidable beach defenses as well as a defense in depth that was to extend inland some twenty miles.

The Allies invaded the south of France on August 15, 1944. This was called Operation Anvil-Dragoon and was second in size only to Operation Overlord, the invasion of Normandy. The 60,000 American assault troops were under the command of United States Generals Lucian K. Truscott and Alexander M. Patch. A Free French division led by General de Lattre de Tassigny also took part in the amphibious assault that was made along a thirty-five-mile stretch of coast between Toulon and Nice. A feature of the airborne landings by parachute troops was the dropping of hundreds of rubber mannequins, or dummies, by Allied troop-carrying planes in areas where paratroops did not actually land. This ruse had been suggested by Miniconi and succeeded in making the Germans think the airborne landings were much larger and more widespread than they actually were.

Shortly before the landings Miniconi was told by Free French headquarters in London to make sure his resistance members were all wearing FFI armbands bearing the Cross of Lorraine to identify themselves to Allied troops coming ashore. This called for a superhuman effort on the part of Claire Miniconi, who was given the task of providing the armbands. First of all, where was she to get the cloth? Wartime shortages had made such material almost unobtainable. Secondly, who was to help her make almost seven hundred armbands? Without hesitation Claire Miniconi enlisted the aid of not only all of the women resistants in the Jean-Marie Group but also dozens of other friends and neighbors. Sheets, pillowcases, towels, and other well-worn pieces of cloth were donated and dozens of volunteer seamstresses went to work to make sure the armbands were ready on time. It was a minor victory in the large-scale war effort and one that would be ignored in the history books, but it was one that Claire Miniconi and her friends vividly remembered after the war.

Cannes: A Threat of Destruction

Cannes was out of the immediate path of the Allied landings, but within a matter of days it too was seriously threatened, not so much by the Allies as by the Germans, who planned to destroy much of the city before they were driven out. When the German defenses in depth began to crumble and the Wehrmacht troops prepared to retreat up the Rhône Valley, Miniconi learned that the German commander in Cannes had received orders to carry out his destruction of the city and then join in the retreat.

The German commander in Cannes was Colonel Erik Schneider. His military occupation force was the German 148th Infantry Division. Miniconi learned of the enemy's plans from a woman tavern owner, Toinette Marcoux. Marcoux overheard a drunken German infantry officer bragging about the demolition plans and relayed the information to Miniconi. When Allied warships in the harbor began to shell the city, Miniconi decided he must act.

Toinette Marcoux told Miniconi that Colonel Schneider came to her tavern every night to eat and drink alone in one of the back rooms. Up to now Miniconi had kept his identity secret in Cannes, although he had worn his FFI armband and openly taken part in aiding the Allies further along the coast. Now, gambling his life, he cast aside all secrecy.

On a night in late August Miniconi entered Toinette Marcoux's tavern. The front-bar area was filled with German troops, but Marcoux nodded her head toward a door leading to the back room where Colonel Schneider was eating a sparse meal. As the Allies closed in on the city, food became almost unobtainable. Schneider's meal on this night was a plate of plain spaghetti.

Miniconi approached the door to the private room and entered without knocking. Schneider was indeed alone and did not look up. Miniconi pulled up a chair and sat down across the table from the colonel. There was a moment's silence and then Miniconi identified himself as Jean-Marie, the man in charge of the resistance in the Cannes area.

Still Colonel Schneider did not look up, but went on eating his sauceless spaghetti.

Miniconi then told Schneider that the resistance had learned that the Wehrmacht's 148th Infantry Division planned to destroy all of the public buildings, utilities, and hotels in the city before it withdrew.

Schneider did not reply.

Miniconi went on to say that neither he nor any of the resistance would stand by and allow such mass destruction. Then he appealed to Schneider as a German officer. Such wanton destruction was not only uncivilized but it would accomplish nothing in the way of delaying the Allies.

Schneider looked up for the first time.

Miniconi then presented his proposition. If Schneider would give him his word as a soldier and officer not to carry out his demolition orders, Miniconi's resistance group would promise him safe conduct out of the city. If not, Miniconi would order his resistance group to attack—and who knew what unnecessary bloodshed would result.

But Schneider had gone back to eating his spaghetti.

Miniconi waited a few moments. Then he turned and walked out of the room, expecting at any moment to be shot in the back. But no shot was fired and no alarm was sounded to the German soldiers in the bar. Miniconi made his way out of the tavern unmolested. Then he returned home and waited.

The following morning at 3:00 A.M. Miniconi and his wife were awakened by Toinette Marcoux. She was bearing a message from Colonel Schneider. The colonel wanted to meet Miniconi, alone, at the Hotel Splendide. Miniconi and his wife feared that this might be a trap, but Miniconi could not refuse the bait.

Cannes Is Saved

Miniconi met the colonel at the Hotel Splendide a short time later. Except for the proprietor, Schneider was alone. Still without speaking, Colonel Schneider led Miniconi into the hotel basement. There Schneider pointed out a huge metal box with electric wires leading from it to conduits that carried the wires outside the building. Miniconi scarcely needed to be told that this was the master control point for detonating all of the explosive charges that had been put in place throughout the city.

Colonel Schneider handed Miniconi a pair of wire cutters and pointed at the main cable that led from the metal box to the detonator's plunger nearby. Then the colonel wheeled about and left, saying that he was not interested in a safe conduct out of the city: He would remain with his men.

Hesitating only a moment, Miniconi cut the cable leading from the detonator to the metal box master control. Later Miniconi found a diagram in the basement that indicated where all of the conduits led from the master control. All bridges and much of the port-area docks as well as fully three-quarters of the main buildings in Cannes had been wired for destruction. Several tons of dynamite had to be removed from these sites by the Allies when they entered the city.

The following day Colonel Schneider and his 148th Infantry Division evacuated Cannes just a few hours before the Allies entered. They were met by Miniconi and his Jean-Marie Group. All, including Miniconi, were now wearing their FFI armbands.

British historian Peter Leslie, who was the first to tell the story of Miniconi and his Jean-Marie Group, also discovered after the war that Colonel Schneider's gesture that saved the city of Cannes cost him his life. When Schneider and his troops joined the main German forces that were then in full retreat, his superiors confronted him with the fact that the Allies had occupied Cannes without a struggle and that Schneider had failed to carry out his demolition orders. Colonel Schneider was court martialed for dereliction of duty, historian Leslie recorded, and shot by a firing squad.

Curiously, a situation similar to that in Cannes

but on a much larger scale would develop when the Allies approached Paris. There the German commander, General Dietrich von Choltitz, would receive direct orders from Hitler to turn one of the most beautiful cities in the world into "nothing but a field of ruins" to prevent it from falling into the hands of the enemy. As in Cannes, the French resistance would play a key role in influencing the Paris commander in his decision about carrying out Hitler's orders.

IX

The Hedgehog's Homecoming

BETWEEN THE TIME of the successful Allied landings in Normandy and those along the Riviera, Marie-Madeleine, alias Hedgehog, was finally allowed to return to France. She had been pleading for months to do so, but Sir Claude Dansey, her boss at the SOE, insisted she was too well known to the Germans and would immediately be picked up. Finally, however, de Gaulle's Free French intelligence service insisted that Marie-Madeleine was needed to play an active role in the forthcoming liberation of France.

Reluctantly, Dansey allowed Marie-Madeleine to return—but not as the head of Noah's Ark. That organization had been rebuilt and expanded by several other Ark leaders. If she were captured by the Germans, Dansey instructed Marie-Madeleine, she should claim to be a British agent sent by Dansey to learn just how strong the Communist resistance organization was in Paris so the Allies would know how to deal with it when they freed the French capital.

German intelligence knew that Dansey was in immediate charge of all British agents, and he believed the Gestapo would deal less severely with Marie-Madeleine if they thought she was such an agent rather than a resistance leader. Just why Dansey thought so is not clear since British agents caught by the Gestapo had been dealt with brutally.

Marie-Madeleine accepted Dansey's suggestion but recognized it as a forlorn hope in the event of her capture. What she must do, she knew, was simply not *be* captured. And once back in France she certainly had every intention of contacting her old Noah's Ark comrades.

Marie-Madeleine was well aware of the odds against her remaining free once she was back in France. Casualties among agents sent into France by the American, British, and French secret services ran at over forty percent. But these were simply statistics. She did not believe they applied to her. No agent ever did. Confidently and with great anticipation Marie-Madeleine prepared for what she considered her homecoming.

She returned not by parachute or Lysander light aircraft but by Hudson small bomber. The plane arrived over its destination, the forest of Fontainebleau, at midnight. Despite the bright moonlight, Marie-Madeleine could see beneath them the blinking flashlights that indicated it was safe for the pilot to land. Such signal lights were directed straight upward by placing a flashlight in a long metal sleeve so its light could be visible only from above and not by anyone on the ground.

In heavily populated areas where it was too risky to use any lights at all no matter how well they were shielded, some agents were equipped with a radio device called Eureka. Eureka, from the Greek word meaning "I have found it," was invented by the British. It gave out a sound signal that directed pilots toward a landing area. Late in the war the British also developed what was called the S-phone, the S standing for Secret. With the S-phone an agent on the ground and a pilot flying overhead could actually carry on a conversation at distances up to thirty miles without fear of detection. Neither of these devices, however, was in use at Hedgehog's homecoming.

The landing was made without incident in a

large clearing in the forest. She was surprised to be greeted heartily by Flying Fish (Raymond Pezet), a member of Noah's Ark and an old friend. Her return was to have been secret, she thought. How Pezet happened to be on hand she never learned.

Marie-Madeleine had two pieces of luggage, a suitcase carrying her clothing and personal belongings, and a bird cage containing a carrier pigeon. Pezet suggested they keep the pigeon for a future meal, but Marie-Madeleine dutifully released it and the bird circled and headed back to England. In a cartridge on its leg it bore a message to Dansey announcing her safe arrival. The Hudson bomber was also winging its way to England, having taken off after only a few moments on the ground. Pezet now picked up Marie-Madeleine's suitcase, and they started off through the forest. Hedgehog was home.

Marie-Madeleine told Pezet she wanted to meet with Captain des Isnards (code name Grand Duke, after a champion show dog), who was now running the Noah's Ark network. Pezet said Grand Duke wanted to rendezvous with her too. Almost a week later, having eluded numerous German patrols and station guards, they arrived by train in Aix, the current Ark headquarters near Marseilles.

Grand Duke was delighted to see Marie-Madeleine, and he immediately began to spew forth a long list of the supplies and money needed by the network. She felt as if she had never left home. Radio contact was made with London, and Marie-Madeleine personally relayed Grand Duke's request. No comment was made by Dansey about Marie-Madeleine's resumption of her old role, but a week later several tons of the requested supplies and a suitcase filled with francs were parachuted into the Ark's prearranged drop zone.

Marie-Madeleine was quartered in what was believed to be a safe house in Aix. Grand Duke and his wife were living in a farm outside the town. After the supply drop from London, Grand Duke visited Marie-Madeleine to warn her to be on the lookout for the local Gestapo, who were about to conduct a house-to-house search for resistants. The Germans had been alerted to the imminent landings by the Allies in southern France and were attempting to clear out all resistants in their rear. Grand Duke even encouraged Marie-Madeleine to return with him to his farm, but she refused. She had work to do.

Her work was encoding a series of messages to London bringing the SOE up to date on Ark activities and the status of the resistance throughout southern France. She was in the midst of this work when someone knocked at the front door.

Shoving the "grids," or encoded messages, under the couch, Marie-Madeleine went to the door and opened it. On her doorstep were several Gestapo officers and a dozen German troops. They were searching for an enemy agent, they said, a man who had been seen entering her house.

Capture!

It soon became clear from the description that the man they were searching for was Grand Duke. When Marie-Madeleine insisted there was no man with her and never had been, they still searched the house. They found no one, of course, and were about to leave when one of the Gestapo officers suddenly spun around on his heel and walked over to the couch. Reaching under it, he triumphantly pulled out the coded messages on which Marie-Madeleine had been working. Hedgehog was about to become one of those dread statistics in which she had so steadfastly refused to believe.

Her interrogation began in the house where she was arrested. Fortunately, the Gestapo did not know who she was. It was Grand Duke whom they had come to accept as the head of the Alliance or Noah's Ark, and it was Grand Duke they were after. Following Dansey's advice, Marie-Madeleine now tried to pass herself off as an agent recently parachuted into France. She refused to give them her name, saying she would only identify herself to the Gestapo commander. Immediately one of the Gestapo officers tried to talk her into becoming a double agent. Stalling for time, Marie-Madeleine seemed to be considering the offer. She even hinted she might be able to lead them to Grand Duke. Nevertheless, she was taken to the local military jail, a former barracks that the Germans had recently remodeled to house resistance suspects.

Fortunately, the Gestapo commander was not in Aix and was not due until the next day. But when he did arrive, Marie-Madeleine knew, it would only be a matter of time before he learned who she was: Hedgehog, the long-sought head of Noah's Ark, a prize catch. Then the torture would begin. Would she be able to stand up under it, or would she break and betray Grand Duke and all of the others in the rebuilt network? Briefly she thought of suicide. Her cyanide pills were still concealed in her handbag. Then she put the thought out of her mind. She must first try to escape.

Marie-Madeleine lay on her cot in her solitary cell until midnight when the silence in the guard room indicated the guards had fallen asleep. Then in the pitch dark she made her way to the barred cell window. The window opened on to a narrow alley, and her cell was on the first floor. In order to see what lay immediately below the barred window she moved her cot and stood on it. She could see very little in the dim light, but no one seemed to be about.

Escape!

Marie-Madeleine tested the bars. They were solidly set in the cement of the newly installed window frame. A sledgehammer and a crow bar would be needed to remove them. But then she noted a curious thing. The spaces between the bars did not seem to be uniform. Two bars were more widely spaced than the others. The difference in the gaps was not much, perhaps an inch or two, but there was a difference. Could she squeeze herself between them?

Certainly she would not be able to do so while fully dressed. Quickly she slipped out of her dress, her underclothes, and her shoes. Leaving her shoes and underclothes behind her, Marie-Madeleine clutched her dress in the hand she thrust through the window. Then she tried to thrust her head through. It was impossible. Her head would not "give" as the rest of her body might if she squeezed that far.

But she *must* make it. Jamming her head forward as hard as she could, she felt blood trickle down her face as her ears were torn by the restricting bars. But her head was outside the window! Now she had begun to sweat and the perspiration had lubricated her naked body as if she had been oiled for her escape attempt.

The next hardest part was her hips. This effort too seemed impossible, but she turned sideways so her belly and her buttocks would flatten out against the bars. Wiggling and thrusting fiercely, she squeezed the bottom half of her body the rest of the way and dropped to the pavement below with a dull thump.

For a few moments she lay quietly in true hedgehog fashion, doubled up in a ball. The fall had knocked her partially unconscious, but she also wanted to remain out of the line of sight of any guard who might shine a light her way from the end of the alley.

Finally she roused herself enough to pull her dress over her head. A naked woman running through the streets would *certainly* create a sensation, she thought. As it was, a barefooted one out alone during curfew would be conspicuous enough. Cautiously, she made her way step by step out of the alley and onto a side street.

She walked slowly but purposefully. Somehow she must make her way to Grand Duke's farm. And dawn would soon be breaking, heightening her need to get as far as possible from the barracks jail before the guards awakened and discovered her escape.

Marie-Madeleine knew where the farm was under normal circumstances, but how to get there via back streets and alleys presented a serious problem. Nevertheless, she walked steadily in what she believed to be the correct direction. Along the way she passed a cemetery and decided to rest there briefly, hoping a priest might help her. But she encountered no priest nor even a gravedigger, so again she went on her way. By now it was daylight.

Once she was out of the town and on a road she recognized, Marie-Madeleine began to walk more rapidly. Then, ahead of her and approaching the town, she saw a platoon of soldiers. She quickly solved this problem by joining some peasant women working in a field. Once the soldiers had gone, she gathered up a few sheaves of grain to carry in her arms as if she were taking them home, and again proceeded along the road.

It took Marie-Madeleine until mid-morning to reach Grand Duke's farm. Moments after she arrived and surprised Grand Duke and his wife inside the farmhouse, Marie-Madeleine fell in a faint on the kitchen floor.

After she had been revived by the startled couple, Marie-Madeleine was taken to another safe house by the Grand Duke. He himself remained there with her in hiding because by now the alarm had been sounded for both of them throughout the district, and the Gestapo was in hot pursuit.

They remained in hiding for several weeks. Each night Grand Duke's wife brought them food. Then one night she also brought them the electrifying news that the invasion of southern France had begun.

A few days later Marie-Madeleine and Grand Duke left their safe house and joined the Maquis, who were beginning to arise throughout all of the rural areas and attack the retreating Germans. From one of the Maquis headquarters Marie-Madeleine was able to radio Dansey at the SOE in London that she and Grand Duke were safe.

By now the Allies had broken out of their Normandy beachhead and the race for Paris was on. United States General George Patton and his armored columns had led the beachhead breakout on a wide swing to the south and east of Paris. His eventual goal, however, was not the French capital but the northern provinces of Alsace and Lorraine.

Dansey offered his congratulations to Marie-Madeleine and Grand Duke on their good fortune. He also requested them to head north to Alsace and Lorraine so they could supply Patton with German Order of Battle information before he arrived there.

The co-leaders of Noah's Ark would much rather have taken part in the liberation of Paris. Nevertheless, they complied with Dansey's request. They moved north and began to supply valuable intelligence information to the fiery Patton and his hard-charging armored forces. They continued in this role until the whole of France was freed.

The Freedom Bar

After the war it was learned that it was no accident that the bars in the window of Marie-Madeleine's cell were not evenly spaced. This same flaw occurred in remodeled jails or barracks jails throughout France, especially if local labor was used by the Germans. After French stonemasons had installed the cement windows and iron bars, and their work was duly inspected, a worker would manage to return while the cement was still wet and had not yet set and gently spread two of the bars farther apart than the others. So widespread was this clandestine practice that the stonemasons even had a name for the results of their work. They called it *The Freedom Bar*.

X

The Boy on the Red, White, and Blue Bicycle

THE LIBERATION OF Paris was not a simple military exercise involving a powerful attacking force driving out a weak defending force. If this had been all there was to it, Paris would not have presented much of a problem. The advancing Allied armies with their overwhelming air support far outnumbered the German defensive garrison. In addition, within the city there were thousands of French resistance fighters ready to rise up against the Germans.

But there were several other key parts to the problem.

The Allies did not particularly want to capture Paris immediately.

General de Gaulle *did* want to capture Paris immediately. But *he* did not want the resistance fighters inside the city to rise up until he entered it.

The Allies did not want de Gaulle and his Free French army to attack Paris at all. They hoped the Germans would agree to declare the French capital an "open city" and simply move all of their troops out. Then the Allies could occupy it without bloodshed or destruction.

But German dictator Adolf Hitler would have no part in declaring Paris an open city. The Germans would either continue to occupy it, or they would destroy it. The Allies believed he meant what he said.

Warsaw, the capital of Poland, had faced a similar situation just a few weeks earlier. With Russian liberating forces approaching Warsaw from the east, the Nazi garrison was also threatened by an insurrection of Polish partisans within the city. Before evacuating Warsaw, the German rearguard troops killed some 200,000 Poles and then burned the city to the ground.

How were the Allies to prevent Paris from suffering a similar fate?

Just two weeks before the outbreak of fighting for the liberation of Paris began, German General Dietrich von Choltitz arrived in the City of Light. Before leaving Germany to take over command of the French capital, von Choltitz had received a direct oral order from Hitler: If the Allies attacked Paris, or there was a resistance uprising, he was to completely destroy the city. "Nothing must be left standing," the Führer had said, "no church, no artistic monument, nothing."

General von Choltitz looked like the comic version of a Prussian general. He was a little, round, fat man who wore a monocle and sweated a lot. But there was nothing comic about him. Early in the war as a lieutenant colonel, von Choltitz had lead an attack on the Netherlands—a country on which Germany had not bothered to declare war—which completely destroyed the port city of Rotterdam and caused almost 100,000 Dutch casualties. Later he had fought against the Russians. At Sevastopol, a port on the Black Sea, he ordered his regiment to take no prisoners. When the Germans captured the port city, thousands of Russians were simply massacred. When the Wehrmacht was forced to retreat from Russia, von Choltitz's forces adopted a scorched-earth policy, burning every village and town they passed through. Now he was charged with a similar mission in Paris.

Von Choltitz made his headquarters in the Hotel Meurice. On his second morning there, after a hearty breakfast—Parisians, of course, were literally starving—he stood on the balcony of his suite staring down at the quiet street. As he watched, a lone boy of perhaps eleven or twelve came riding slowly along on a bicycle. Von Choltitz looked at him almost fondly, thinking of his own family back in Germany. One of his own sons was about this boy's age. (After the fall of Paris and von Choltitz's capture he described his first sight of the boy to Allied newsmen.)

Then von Choltitz became aware of the boy's bicycle. It was freshly painted, a rare sight in this city of wartime shortages. But it was the colors that really caught the general's eye. The bicycle's frame was painted blue, its front mudguard white, and its rear mudguard red. The French national colors. (That they were also the American national colors did not occur to the general. This was a French boy. There could be no doubt about that.)

The smile faded from General von Choltitz's face. As he watched, the boy circled about and again rode past the hotel. The boy was well dressed in a dark blue smock. Now he looked up and saw the general standing on the balcony. Then the boy reached inside his smock, pulled out a small French tricolor flag and waved it back and forth. Von Choltitz quickly left the balcony and went to summon an aide. But by the time the aide came and von Choltitz had taken him out onto the balcony, the boy on the red, white, and blue bike with his French flag of defiance had disappeared in the maze of Paris streets. This was not the last time he was to be seen during the next several weeks, however.

"Paris Will Be Bypassed"

Elsewhere in Paris on that same day Colonel Claude Olliver (code name Jade Amicol), the head of British intelligence in Paris, received a hand-delivered message from the SOE in London. "The Allied Command," the message said, "is determined to bypass Paris and delay its liberation as long as possible. Nothing, repeat, nothing must be allowed to happen that will change these plans."

Knowing full well that the Germans intended to destroy Paris if it were attacked, Colonel Olliver should have been delighted at the word of Allied intentions. Instead, he regarded the bypassing of Paris by the Allied armies as a catastrophe. The reason: There were at least 25,000 Communist resistants in the city, and even though they were only lightly armed it would be next to impossible to prevent their rising in a full-scale revolt against the occupying forces.

Once such an insurrection began it would be joined by thousands of other resistants pouring into the city from the surrounding countryside. It would be Warsaw all over again. The Germans would not only carry on a house-to-house defense but they would also slaughter countless resistants and civilians in the process. In addition, the Germans would begin the wholesale demolition of every historic building and monument as well as the several aqueducts which supplied all of the city's water supply and some forty-five bridges across the Seine River. With the destruction of the bridges Paris would become merely several islands of scorched earth surrounded by loops of the Seine.

By late August of 1944 Paris was partially encircled by American armored and infantry divisions. Within the city was a German rearguard of between 20,000 and 25,000 fully armed mechanized troops. These troops composed an infantry division plus numerous batteries of anti-aircraft guns, which could and probably would be used as anti-tank guns. Von Choltitz was certain that the Allies would never bomb Paris. He was right. But the Allies did not plan to fight for Paris either, or at least not right away. They planned to circle around it and drive the Germans out of the rest of France first. Then they would occupy Paris at their leisure.

From a military standpoint the Allied strategy was sound. Both General Dwight Eisenhower and General Bernard Montgomery, the American and British top commanders, agreed that to occupy Paris at this stage of the campaign would bog down the Allied offensive. Several divisions—perhaps as many as eight—would be needed to take and hold the city. And then a major portion of the Allied supply effort would be needed simply to feed the civilian populace.

The Red Ball Express

By now the French resistance along with Allied bombing efforts had virtually destroyed the country's railway system. Consequently, supplies were moved via the unique "Red Ball Express." This was a trucking system that operated twenty-four hours a day from Normandy to front-line supply depots. Nothing was allowed to slow its operation. If a truck broke down, it was simply shoved off the road and abandoned. Shifts of trucking crews were changed at each end of the run, a round-trip distance of more than four hundred miles from Normandy to Paris. But all of the Red

Ball Express supplies were sorely needed—especially gasoline—by the fighting forces if the Allies were to reach Germany before the summer was out.

The decision to bypass Paris was, General Eisenhower declared, a cruel but necessary one. Churchill and Roosevelt agreed. All of these leaders, however, reckoned without two vital elements: Charles de Gaulle and the French resistance.

Communists Versus De Gaulle

De Gaulle, of course, knew that Paris was a stronghold of Communist resistants. He also knew that if they were instrumental in driving the Germans out and took over control of the city, his chances of establishing a government under himself would be seriously threatened. The Communists were not loyal to de Gaulle and France. They were loyal to Russia. To prevent a Communist takeover, de Gaulle had decided, Paris must be liberated from the outside, not from within, and he must enter with the liberating forces or shortly thereafter.

Even before the Normandy invasion de Gaulle had taken two important steps to weaken the Communist resistance in Paris and strengthen his own cause. With the approach of D-Day, the SOE had stepped up its weapons drops to all of the resistance networks so their members would be fully armed when they rose up against the Germans. At de Gaulle's insistence most of these weapons were parachuted to the Maquis and other resistants in outlying areas and only a handful were consigned to Paris.

That this procedure was justified by motivations other than de Gaulle's personal ones was clearly indicated by the fact that in the peninsula of Brittany alone fewer than 100,000 FFI kept several German divisions pinned down during the Normandy campaign. In the whole of France, it was estimated by General Eisenhower, the FFI's efforts in preventing German troops from attacking the Allied invasion forces were the equivalent of some fifteen Allied divisions. As always, these resistance efforts were not without cost. The Germans were now desperate, and their reprisals were even more savage than before. In March of 1944 an entire Maquis band numbering more than a thousand resistants was wiped out in the Haute Savoie region. In July another Maquis force of similar size was destroyed at Vercors.

The De Gaulle Solution

De Gaulle's second step was to create a general staff outside France for the French Forces of the

Interior, the FFI, within France. This command structure placed the French military forces on an equal footing with those of the United States, Great Britain, and Canada within the framework of the Supreme Headquarters Allied Expeditionary Forces (SHAEF). As head of this newly created general staff de Gaulle named General Pierre Koenig to coordinate all resistance activities within France shortly before and after the Allied invasion. General Eisenhower, SHAEF commander, cooperated by accepting Koenig on an equal footing with the several other national commanders. Even more importantly, Eisenhower authorized the formation of an all-French combat division to be commanded by French General Jacques-Philippe Leclerc. This unit was named the French Second Armored Division, more commonly called *Division Leclerc*.

After the Allies had broken out of their Normandy beachhead and the race for Paris begun, de Gaulle instructed Koenig to contact the Communist resistance forces within the capital and inform them that Paris would be liberated from without, not within, and the liberators would be Leclerc's French division. De Gaulle made this pronouncement with virtually no authority other than his own. His purpose was twofold: to prevent a Communist resistance uprising within Paris and to put pressure on General Eisenhower to let de Gaulle do exactly as he said he would do, designate the French Second Armored Division under General Leclerc as the immediate liberators of Paris. This grand and symbolic gesture would cement de Gaulle's claim to leadership of the new French nation.

Communist Reaction

The Communist resistance forces within Paris led by Henri Rol-Tanguy reacted to Koenig's news angrily. Their anger was not due solely to the threatened frustration of their own plans to establish a postwar Communist government in France. It was due mainly to the fact that throughout France the FFI was now openly fighting the Germans, but in Paris the FFI was doing nothing. Now, they felt, was the time to strike a blow for freedom.

On August 18 several thousand Paris resistants, many of whom were members of the metropolitan police force, seized the city's police headquarters opposite Notre Dame cathedral and hoisted the French national flag above the building's roof. This was the first time the French tricolor had been flown publicly in Paris since the Germans had marched in in 1940.

On the morning the tricolor was hoisted over police headquarters many people noticed a boy on a red, white, and blue bicycle riding slowly back and forth in the street in front of the building. On the handlebars of the bike was also a tricolor flag. People asked each other who the boy was. Nobody seemed to know.

Almost immediately after the police headquarters takeover, the sound of small-arms fire could be heard throughout the city as other resistants clashed with German troops. Within a matter of hours more than a hundred French resistants and about half that many German soldiers were killed. As the skirmishing spread and Nazi military vehicles began to be ambushed and set ablaze in the Paris streets, General von Choltitz at his Hotel Meurice headquarters began to prepare orders for destroying and then evacuating the city. Von Choltitz delayed immediate action, however, even when the insurrection continued into the following day.

Enter a Man of Peace

It was at this crucial point that a man of peace and sanity entered the drama. He was Raoul Nordling, Sweden's consul-general. Officially a neutral country, Sweden had maintained government offices in Paris all through the war. Raoul Nordling, while also officially a neutral, had many friends in the resistance.

On August 20 Nordling saw von Choltitz and offered to act as a peace-making mediator between the Germans and the resistants. Von Choltitz agreed. In his conversation with the German general, Nordling got the very definite impression that von Choltitz—despite his reputation for brutality—was eagerly looking for a way out of the dilemma. It was clear that von Choltitz did not want to go down in history as the man responsible for the destruction of Paris. Destroying Rotterdam had been one thing. Then it looked as if Germany would win the war. But Rotterdam was not Paris, and it now looked like Germany would lose the war.

Nordling immediately contacted the resistants who had taken over the police headquarters and told them the Germans had asked for a truce. Since the Germans had requested the cease-fire and the resistants were almost out of ammunition anyway, they agreed to a temporary truce. Elsewhere in the city it was more difficult to bring the insurrection under control, but with the help of several resistance members Nordling managed the feat.

But Henri Rol-Tanguy opposed the truce. That

night he worked with the staffs of several underground newspapers to prepare special morning editions. These newspapers were distributed throughout the city at dawn. All were headlined: AUX BARRICADES! (TO THE BARRICADES!) Reminiscent of the French Revolution, this battle cry rallied not only the resistance but also much of the rest of the civilian population of Paris as nothing else could. Men, women, and children poured into the streets and began ripping up the cobblestone pavements and erecting barricades from behind which they prepared to fight the enemy. They had few weapons. Old World War I rifles had been brought out of hiding, and homemade bombs were prepared to be used against tanks.

The Nobel Bomb-maker

One of the people who manufactured these homemade bombs was a world-renowned scientist, Frédéric Joliot-Curie. Some of Joliot-Curie's prewar experiments on the splitting of the atom and the subsequent chain reaction were to lead to the development of the atom bomb and earn him the Nobel prize. Now, in his basement hideaway, Communist resistant Joliot-Curie was busy turning out much more primitive but nevertheless highly deadly "Molotov cocktails" (crude incendiary grenades named after Russia's V.M. Molotov).

Marie and Pierre Curie had discovered radium in their Paris laboratory early in the century. Their discovery was to aid in the fight against cancer. Now their son-in-law, Joliot-Curie, was using chemicals he had smuggled from their laboratory, where he still worked in peacetime, to make weapons to fight the cancer of Nazi oppression. These handmade grenades were rapidly distributed to resistants throughout the city.

That afternoon another young Communist resistant, André Tollet, led a band of teenagers who took over the Paris City Hall. As soon as they occupied the building several German tanks arrived on the scene and began firing point blank at the youthful defenders barricaded inside. Before Tollet could stop her, a teenage girl resistant, a Joliot-Curie Molotov cocktail in hand, dashed out of the building, ran up to the lead tank and smashed the grenade against the vehicle's turret. As she dashed away she was cut down by gunfire from the other tanks. But the lead tank blew up when the grenade exploded and the other tanks soon retreated.

Looking out the window of City Hall, Tollet also saw another lone figure—a boy on a brightly painted bicycle bearing a tricolor flag. Tollet later

commented that he marveled that the boy on the
bike was not also cut down by the enemy fire.

Ike's Command Decision

Meanwhile, General de Gaulle had been kept
up-to-date on the Paris crisis by General Koenig
via shortwave radio. On his own de Gaulle had
established his headquarters in the nearby city of
Rennes. On August 21 de Gaulle sent a note to
General Eisenhower all but demanding that Allied
troops be sent into Paris to prevent the disaster
that was imminent there. Then de Gaulle sent a
second note. This one was to General Leclerc. It
ordered Leclerc to be prepared to move the Second Armored Division—if necessary without au-
thorization from SHAEF. Leclerc, stationed just
a few miles outside of Paris at Argentan, had already made up his mind to take exactly such action.

Eisenhower's reaction to de Gaulle's strong
note was not as violent as the aides of the sharp-
tempered SHAEF commander thought it would
be. As a military man and a staunch patriot himself, "Ike" had always admired de Gaulle and his
stubborn fight against almost overwhelming odds.
Now Ike read the note, seemed deep in thought
for several moments—he too, of course, was well

aware of the tense Paris situation—and then wrote across the note's face: "It looks as though we shall be compelled to go to Paris."

From that moment things began to happen quickly. Ike also agreed, finally, that General Leclerc and the French Second Armored Division should lead the way into Paris. But he was taking no chances. The battle-tested U.S. Fourth Infantry Division was ordered to back up Leclerc.

After the truce was broken in Paris, fighting again broke out all over the city. It reached a peak on August 23. That afternoon von Choltitz summoned Raoul Nordling to the Hotel Meurice and asked him why neither he nor anybody else seemed to be able to control the FFI. Nordling's response was that the FFI flatly refused to take orders from anybody but de Gaulle and they were not too good about taking orders from him by long distance. Perhaps they would heed de Gaulle in person.

Von Choltitz nodded his head. Then he told Nordling that in that case it was about time to summon de Gaulle to Paris.

Nordling, of course, was astonished at von Choltitz's words, but he wasted no time in questioning them. Instead he asked the German general to make out a pass so Nordling could make his way through the German lines to de Gaulle's headquarters. Immediately von Choltitz made out such a pass authorizing "R. Nordling" to travel through the defense perimeter.

Good fortune now seemed to be smiling on the effort to save Paris, this time in the sheer happenstance of von Choltitz writing not "Raoul Nordling" but "R. Nordling" on the pass. Back in his consular office and preparing to start on his mission, Raoul Nordling suffered a heart attack. The attack did not prove fatal, but it did put him out of action for several weeks. Coincidently, Raoul's brother, Rolf Nordling, was also a consular staff member, and it was he who used the "R. Nordling" pass to reach de Gaulle's headquarters. He arrived there simultaneously with the news from Eisenhower that the French would lead the way back into the French capital.

Paris was liberated on August 25, 1944. As the French entered one side of the city, the Germans left on the other, leaving behind only a few snipers, a small security force, and General von Choltitz.

Enter Le Grand Charles

General Leclerc's tanks and motorized infantry were followed to the outskirts of the city by General de Gaulle riding in a jeep. But de Gaulle refused to enter Paris in a foreign-made car. In the suburbs he climbed out of the jeep and ordered an aide to find him a French vehicle. Somehow this was accomplished. Then de Gaulle rode triumphantly through the streets of the French capital, his arms spread upward in a huge V-for-victory sign. His return was hailed by throngs of men, women, and children cheering de Gaulle, who had helped set them free.

The French soldiers entering the city with de Gaulle were almost overwhelmed by the riotous crowds. Many of the soldiers had relatives living in or near Paris, and the soldiers gave the people swarming around them notes with the names and phone numbers of their relatives and pleaded with them to call and report their safety.

Death on Deliverance Day

But there were also personal tragedies on this otherwise joyous day. Historian Schoenbrun tells of one young tank officer, a Lieutenant Bureau, who left his tank, ran to a nearby phone and called his parents, who were overjoyed to hear his voice. A short time later Lieutenant Bureau was dead, killed by a German sniper. Actually more than a hundred French soldiers and civilians died on the day Paris was liberated, and more than seven hundred were wounded. Almost thirty Germans were killed and more than two hundred wounded.

De Gaulle immediately went to his old office in the Ministry of War. From there he demanded to know what had happened to General von Choltitz. Von Choltitz, it turned out, had risked being shot when he refused to surrender to the FFI. As a military man he said he would only surrender to the French military forces. In this he was obliged by a young French officer, Lieutenant Henri Karcher. Von Choltitz was later led before de Gaulle to sign the official surrender document, which was made out not to the Allies nor even to the French but to the French Forces of the Interior, since they were the only official government-in-being at the time. At first de Gaulle objected to this, but later he admitted its justification.

While the surrender document was being signed, hundreds of thousands of Paris citizens stood in the streets and shouted, "De Gaulle! De Gaulle! De Gaulle!"—to which General Charles de Gaulle did not object. There could now be little doubt in any of the Allied leaders' minds about who would be the future president of the Republic of France.

Last-Minute Resistants

In the cheering crowds were hundreds of French civilians wearing FFI armbands. Most of these people had not actually taken part in resistance activity during the war. They were scornfully referred to by true resistance members as "Resistants of the Last Minute," or "Resistants of August." But the true resistants, at least for the time being, did little to sort out the legitimate members of the FFI from the illegitimate. That day would come sometime in the very near future, as would the day for retribution against collaborationists. Today there was more than enough glory to go around.

And the boy on the red, white, and blue bicycle with its tricolor flag—what about him? Nobody ever found out who he was or what became of him. After the liberation of Paris stories about him grew. It turned out that dozens and dozens of people had seen him, but his identity was unknown. General von Choltitz was one of the first to ask his Allied captors about the boy, but his identity was also a mystery to them. It remains a mystery to this day.

Bibliography

Avni, Haim. *Spain, the Jews and Franco*. New York: The Jewish Publication Society of America, 1982.

Foot, M.R. and J.M. Langley. *MI-9 Escape and Evasion: 1939–1945*. Boston and Toronto: Little, Brown and Company, 1979–1980.

Fourcade, Marie-Madeleine. *Noah's Ark: The Secret Underground*. New York: E.P. Dutton, 1974.

Howarth, Patrick. *Undercover*. Boston: Routledge & Kegan Paul, 1980.

Johnson, Brian. *The Secret War*. New York: Methuen, 1978.

Kersaudy, François. *Churchill and De Gaulle*. New York: Atheneum, 1982.

Keegan, John. *Six Armies in Normandy*. New York: The Viking Press, 1982.

Lawson, Don. *The Secret World War II*. New York: Franklin Watts, 1978.

_____. *An Album of World War II: Homefronts*. New York: Franklin Watts, 1980.

Lay, Beirne, Jr. *Presumed Dead*. New York: Dodd, Mead and Company, 1980.

Leslie, Peter. *The Liberation of the Riviera*. New York: Wyndham Books, 1980.

Marshall, Bruce. *The White Rabbit*. Boston: Houghton Mifflin, 1953.

Masterman. J.C. *The Double-cross System in the War of 1939 to 1945*. New Haven: Yale University Press, 1972.

Popov, Dusko. *Spy/Counter Spy*. London: Weidenfeld and Nicholson, 1974.

Pryce-Jones, David. *Paris in the Third Reich*. New York: Holt, Rinehart and Winston, 1981.

Rhodes, Anthonus. *Propaganda–The Art of Persuasion: World War II*. New York and London: Chelsea House, 1976.

Russell, Francis. *The Secret War*. Alexandria, Virginia: Time-Life Books, 1981.

Schoenbrun, David. *Soldiers of the Night*. New York: E.P. Dutton, 1980.

Stevenson, William. *A Man Called Intrepid*. New York: Harcourt Brace Jovanovich, 1976.

Wilkinson, James D. *The Intellectual Resistance in Europe*. Cambridge: Harvard University Press, 1981.

Winterbottom, F.W. *The Ultra Secret*. New York: Harper & Row, 1974.

Index

About the Author

During World War II, Don Lawson spent three years overseas in Great Britain and on the European continent with the counterintelligence branch of the Ninth Air Force. Since then he has maintained a keen interest in and has written several books on various aspects of wartime intelligence activities. He also has a war library of several thousand volumes.

He has a Doctor of Literature degree from Cornell College in Iowa and attended the University of Iowa's Writers Workshop. He is also the former editor-in-chief of two encyclopedias for young people—*Compton's* and *The American Educator*. He now devotes all of his working time to writing books for young people.